You're invited to a

CREEPOVER™

The House Next Door

SIMON SPOTLIGHT

written by P. J. Night

SIMON SPOTLIGHT
New York London Toronto Sydney New Delhi

This book is a work of fiction. Any references to historical events, real people, or real places are used fictitiously. Other names, characters, places, and events are products of the author's imagination, and any resemblance to actual events or places or persons, living or dead, is entirely coincidental.

SIMON SPOTLIGHT

An imprint of Simon & Schuster Children's Publishing Division

1230 Avenue of the Americas, New York, New York 10020

Copyright © 2013 by Simon & Schuster, Inc.

All rights reserved, including the right of reproduction in whole or in part in any form.

SIMON SPOTLIGHT and colophon are registered trademarks of Simon & Schuster, Inc.

YOU'RE INVITED TO A CREEPOVER is a trademark of Simon & Schuster, Inc.

Text by Rebecca Frazer

For information about special discounts for bulk purchases, please contact Simon & Schuster Special Sales at 1-866-506-1949 or business@simonandschuster.com.

Manufactured in the United States of America 0214 OFF

First Edition 10 9 8 7 6 5 4 3 2

ISBN 978-1-4424-8233-3

ISBN 978-1-4424-8234-0 (eBook)

Library of Congress Control Number 2012956188

PROLOGUE

December 27th

"Only a few more days now," the boy announced to his brother one gloomy, late December afternoon. The clouds hung low overhead, threatening to rain at any moment. The holidays were over (not that they meant much to him anymore), and New Year's Eve was fast approaching. Despite the weather outside, the boy felt lighter and happier than he had in years. The only thing weighing him down at this moment was just how much still needed to be done. No detail could be left to chance. Timing was everything.

"Yeah," his brother replied, but the boy could tell he wasn't all that excited.

The boy turned and glared at him. "What?"

His brother looked down, studying his shoes. "Nothing. It's just—"

"Oh no," interrupted the boy. "Don't even start with this again. We're going through with it."

His brother scratched his cheek and shook his head, letting out a long sigh. He paced back and forth on the worn floorboards that creaked beneath his feet, finally stopping to gaze out the window. The air was thick with the approaching storm, and, as usual, he felt like he was suffocating. It was the time of year that he felt the most cooped up, but was that enough reason to go through with the plan?

"So, are you in or out?" the boy prodded. "I mean, I could do it alone, but you'll regret it. I know you will."

"Just let me think," his brother snapped. He was tired of this constant pressure. He just needed more time to decide, and time unfortunately was running out. "It's just such a big decision. Do we really want to do this to other people? They seem so nice. . . ."

"But it's *our* turn," the boy was quick to reply. "And it's now or never."

At that moment, as though on cue, lightning streaked

across the sky. A crack of thunder followed right after. The storm was right on top of them. As the first drops of rain began to pelt down, the boy's brother turned to him. There were risks, sure, but the boy was right. Now was the time. Slowly, his brother began nodding.

CHAPTER 1

December 31st

"I'm glad it will be dark by the time our guests arrive," Alyssa Peterson remarked to her sister and mom as they drove down their quiet, one-lane street. "That way nobody will have to see that house."

"It looks creepier than usual today," Amanda replied. "At least in the summer it's hidden behind the trees."

"I wish the town would just tear it down once and for all," Mrs. Peterson agreed as she turned to pull into their driveway, kicking up dust in their trail. Their last-minute trip to the grocery store for a few missing party items had resulted in bags and bags of must-have snacks. She gently leaned on the horn. A second later her youngest daughter, Anne, bounded out of the house to help unload the car.

The girls were almost finished bringing the bags inside when Alyssa motioned for her two younger sisters to huddle around her.

"Everyone at the party tonight will probably want to hear stories about the house next door, but let's try not talk about it," she began. "This is going to be our biggest and best New Year's Eve party yet, and for once I'd like the party to be about us and not that thing next door. Agreed?"

As if on cue, all three sisters turned and stared at the house. The house was something they avoided as much as possible. Its facade was in shambles—glass was cracked on some of the windows, shingles often blew off the roof, and paint was stripped from the wooden boards that loosely held the house together—but they had heard the inside was even more decayed. None of the Petersons had actually been inside the house, but according to town gossip, floorboards were rotting away, doors were hanging loosely on rusty hinges, and some of the electrical wiring was dangerously exposed. Judging on the condition of the lawn, it was easy to believe the rumors. An old-fashioned wheelbarrow was overturned and corroded with rust on the dead grass. And a broken light post that stood near the wheelbarrow sometimes flicked and buzzed with a surge of electricity.

The sisters turned back and looked at one another.

"Agreed!" Amanda and Anne said in unison.

"It's almost time, Amanda!" Mrs. Peterson called up the stairs to the second floor. Amanda quickly glanced at the clock on her nightstand and frowned. Her guests would start arriving soon, and she wasn't close to being ready for her family's annual New Year's Eve party. She swiped a tiny brush across her fingernail, adding a final coat of dark berry-red polish.

"Be right down!" Amanda replied. She lightly blew on her fingernails—trying to dry them as quickly as possible—as she walked over to the mirror hanging on the back of her bedroom door for one final chance to examine her outfit before joining her sisters down-stairs. The corner of her mouth tilted slightly upward as she admired her new skirt in the reflection. It was a Christmas present from her younger sister, Anne, and to her surprise, she loved the soft pink color. She twirled around and the skirt's light, airy fabric billowed around her. Smoothing down the ruffles, she looked herself over from head to toe, from the slightly darker pink shirt to the white ballet slippers. *All right,* she thought, *maybe I've gone a little too girly.* She slipped out of her shoes and tugged on her favorite pair of silver-metallic high-top sneakers. As she tied the laces, she started thinking about Paul Furby, hoping that he would finally notice her this year.

"Amanda, we need you downstairs now!" Mrs. Peterson called again.

Amanda swung the door open and stepped into the hallway just as raindrops began pattering on the roof. She ran back into her room and peered out the window. Thick, dark clouds hung heavily over their house. She leaned closer into the window until she could see down to the porch below. After lots and lots of begging by the three sisters, their parents had finally agreed that this year the adults would stay upstairs while the girls would be allowed to host their own party in the basement. It would be guys and girls until midnight, and then the boys would leave. The girls would stay for a sleepover and Mr. Peterson's famous New Year's Day breakfast. Strictly no adults allowed. And the sisters were hoping the mild southern Texas weather would hold throughout the night so they could mingle outside on the porch too. But as Amanda saw the rain streaking down her window, she wondered if they were doomed. She hoped this bit of rain would pass soon.

Slowly, her gaze swept across the wildflower fields and toward the creepy old neighboring house. She could barely even make out its silhouette in the dark night, but her thoughts raced to a memory she'd rather forget.

Months earlier, Amanda had been throwing a softball back and forth with Anne, breaking in her new catcher's mitt. Amanda was always far more athletic than her sisters, so when she tossed the ball to Anne, she didn't expect her sister to hurl it back so forcefully. It went straight over Amanda's head and way past their lawn. After scouring the meadow for the lost ball, Amanda finally found it, and she turned to tell Anne. But when she reached down to pick it up, the ball had disappeared again. Amanda walked a little farther and still couldn't find it. As she walked on, she saw the ball roll out of the tall weeds and into the lifeless yard of the abandoned house—as if something or someone was using the ball to lure her closer to it. When Amanda finally snatched the ball up, she was right next to the house, nearer than she'd ever been. She heard whispers coming from inside. She wasn't sure, but it sounded like they were saying "stay away." She ran back to Anne and told her that she was done playing catch and wanted to go back inside.

The thought of that day still made Amanda uncomfortable. She sighed and decided it was finally time to join her sisters before her mom called her again.

Amanda flew down the stairs. She stopped abruptly when she reached the dining room, blinking her eyes in disbelief. Her parents had transformed their country-style home into a glamorous nightclub. While they were at the grocery store, Mr. Peterson must have swapped the large shabby-chic wooden dining-room table, where the family ate dinner together every night, with three tall glass-and-chrome tables. Amanda ran her finger along the smooth glass as she walked past each table. Her eyes feasted on plates piled high with fresh shrimp and cocktail sauce, sushi, spring rolls, and seven different kinds of dip surrounded by veggies and crackers. There was even a chocolate fountain for dipping fruit and pieces of cake, and a large crystal bowl filled with frothy, pink punch. The Petersons' New Year's Eve party had never been so elaborate.

Ten years earlier, when the Petersons first moved to Glory, Texas, Mr. and Mrs. Peterson had invited a few of their coworkers over to clink glasses at midnight. Every year, as they made more friends, more guests were invited and the party had gotten increasingly impressive. Amanda had never seen her home as luxuriously decorated as it was tonight. This year, it seemed like all of Glory had been invited, and that made them the most famous family in town—at least for tonight.

Then, all of a sudden, the lights went dim. Amanda spun around and watched as speckles of light began to dance on the walls. She looked up to see a giant mirrored disco ball slowly turning above her.

"What do you think?" Anne asked.

The corner of Amanda's mouth lifted and she nodded. "Amazing!"

"Let's grab the snacks," Anne suggested. "Mom's just about finished."

10

Amanda followed her younger sister into the kitchen, where Mrs. Peterson was standing at the counter dipping large, red strawberries into a bowl filled with dark chocolate. She was wearing a bright red dress and black, shiny patent-leather heels. She also wore the earrings Mr. Peterson had hidden in her Christmas stocking. The earrings sparkled in the light. Amanda couldn't help but think her mom looked glamorous, even though she was wearing her old stained apron over her party dress.

Mrs. Peterson glanced at Amanda and grinned. "You look beautiful, Amanda! I knew we could get you out of those old jeans."

"I told Alyssa you'd like my present," Anne said, looking very smug while sitting on a stool at the counter next to their mom. "She said you wouldn't be seen in public wearing it because it's a skirt."

"I do like it." Amanda smiled at her sister. "Are these for us, Mom?" Amanda asked, walking over to a large plate filled with the delicious chocolate-covered strawberries.

"I made them especially for you," Mrs. Peterson said, knowing her middle daughter loved the secret ingredient—a pinch of sea salt in the dark chocolate. The sweet-salty combo was Amanda's favorite indulgence.

"Thanks, Mom," Amanda replied. She grabbed the plate and headed for the basement stairs. Anne wrinkled her nose at the passing strawberries, never really caring much for any kind of fruit—even those covered in chocolate. She hopped off the stool, grabbed a few bottles of soda, and was quickly on Amanda's heels. Mrs. Peterson chuckled and shook her head. Even though her three girls were close in age, they were very different from one another.

Alyssa was twelve; Amanda was eleven; and Anne was ten. It was a family tradition for everyone in the Peterson family to have a first name that started with A. The girls always told their friends it was easy to remember who was oldest because their names lined up in alphabetical order: Alyssa, Amanda, then Anne. Being the oldest, Alyssa was known as the responsible one. Not only was she a straight-A student and on the honor roll, she was also the treasurer of her seventh-grade class and secretary of the Environmental Club. Amanda was in sixth grade and loved to play sports, especially in the warm Texas sun, and was already cocaptain of the varsity volleyball squad. And Anne, the youngest and in fifth grade, was a social butterfly—spunky, fun-loving, and always up for a dare! But as different as they were, they were as close as sisters could be. Also with Anne's recent growth spurt—that added two inches to her height—the girls often overheard people saying that they could pass for triplets.

Amanda entered the basement with Anne close behind her, and she carefully placed the overflowing plate of strawberries next to the rest of the snacks on the coffee table.

"Where have you been?" Alyssa asked. "I've been waiting for you both to help me." She was teetering on a chair, trying to center a gold-and-silver HAPPY NEW YEAR! banner on the wall above the sliding glass doors in the basement. She glanced at her sisters and nearly fell off the chair. She knew Anne couldn't wait to wear her new dress, but she was surprised to see how grown-up her little sister looked in it! Anne spun in a circle and the cream-colored dress twirled around her. Her eyes twinkled just as brightly as the rhinestones on her black velvet belt. She even added a swipe of lip gloss that matched her cheerful poppy-colored cardigan and flats.

Alyssa was equally surprised to see Amanda—one

of the biggest tomboys she knew—wearing a skirt! She was about to say something when a small wobble from the chair snapped her attention back to balancing on it.

"Is this centered?" Alyssa asked, still holding the banner.

Anne stepped back to get a better look, and crossed her arms. "A little to the left," she directed. Alyssa adjusted the banner.

"No, too much! Now an inch down," Anne said.

Alyssa sighed. Her arms ached from holding up the sign. "There!" she declared, putting a thumbtack into it. Crooked or too low, the banner was hung. She leaped off the chair as graceful as a cat—a sure sign of the many years she had spent in the ballet studio.

Alyssa eyed the clock and walked over to a small table to pick up the list she created days earlier. Studying it, she frowned. "Okay, guys, we're now officially running late," she told her sisters. "It's seven twenty, and our guests will start to arrive in about ten minutes." She quickly scanned the goodies on the snack table. "Anne, run upstairs and grab the sparkling cider and plastic champagne flutes. We'll need them to make a toast at midnight."

Alyssa then walked back over to the sliding glass doors and looked outside. "Looks like the rain has stopped. Amanda, you'll need to clean up the porch. Sweep off all the leaves, put some candles around, arrange the chairs in a semicircle, and put the table over there," she said, pointing to the far side of the porch. "And pick some wildflowers from the meadow. We can use them to brighten up the porch."

Amanda shot a look at Anne, and they both rolled their eyes. It always seemed like Alyssa was bossing them around, but they were used to it by now.

"I'll organize the snack table so it doesn't look like a huge mess," Alyssa continued. "Remember, we only have ten minutes. So hurry!"

Amanda grabbed the broom, a couple of old jam jars to use as flower vases, and some tea lights from the cupboard and went out to the porch. Winters in Glory, Texas, were usually sunny and warm during the day, but the temperature could dip when the sun went down. Even so, the Peterson sisters agreed that as long as it didn't rain too much, it would be fun to celebrate outside while the clock ticked toward midnight.

Amanda wiped all the furniture dry and then swept

the leaves away. And although the wooden furniture was now arranged and tidy, it still looked drab. Annoyed that Alyssa had been right about needing flowers to brighten up the porch, Amanda sighed loudly and walked behind the Petersons' house, where she was sure to find some wildflowers in the vast meadow that surrounded their house.

Amanda had always loved smelling the subtle, sweet scent of the wildflowers as she played catch with her dad in the evenings or practiced basketball layups in the driveway. The colorful fields that surrounded their redbrick home made it look just like a picture on a postcard. But she always wished that they lived a little closer to town. Their house was miles away from school, and she always felt so isolated living out in the middle of *nowhere*, as she usually put it. One tiny, winding dirt road was the only way to get to and from the Petersons' house. Sometimes her friends' parents would complain about making the drive for after-school homework sessions and weekend sleepovers. And, to be fair, it really was far from town. Amanda also wished she had neighbors she could visit. Only one house stood along with the Petersons' at the end of the dusty road. And it had been abandoned since before they had even moved to Glory, so it didn't really count.

Amanda remembered noticing earlier that day while it was still light, that the prettiest wildflowers were blooming in the field farthest from their home—and closest to the abandoned house. Amanda bit her bottom lip. She didn't want her sisters to call her chicken, but she also didn't want to get in trouble. Their parents never wanted them roaming too close to the deserted house.

And that was fine with Amanda and Alyssa. They never liked getting too close anyway. It was a strange house. And it always left them feeling uneasy. Vines—dead and brown—enveloped it, making it look like a bug trapped in a spider web. The mailbox hung from its post by a single rusty nail—waiting to be released to its freedom—and creaked at the smallest passing breeze. And, once, she and Alyssa saw the mailbox swinging back and forth on its nail on a perfectly still and cloudless day.

For some reason, only the youngest Peterson sister, Anne, had never been bothered by the house's oddities. She had laughed when her sisters told her that a silly old mailbox had made them run as fast as wild horses back into the safety of their own house. And, of course, they later agreed that there had to be a rational explanation for why the mailbox had swayed back and forth on a windless day. An animal could have scampered across and the girls didn't see it. Still, the thought of anything having to do with the house sent a chill down Amanda's spine.

As Amanda reached the wildflowers, she thought about that eerie day, and her heart thumped rapidly in her chest. She quickly gathered the prettiest flowers, willing herself not to look over at the old house. The basket she was carrying was just about filled when she heard a screeching sound. Amanda cringed. She couldn't resist it any longer. She looked up toward the house.

There it stood, forbidding as always, surrounded by the same dead trees. Amanda held her breath as she waited for more sounds to come from the direction of the house. There were none. Amanda puffed out her cheeks while exhaling with relief. But her muscles quickly tightened as she noticed something about the house that sent a cold shock through her veins. The shutters on the attic window, which had been tightly closed and locked ever since the Petersons moved to Glory, were suddenly wide open. The window, now exposed to the world, stared dark and bleak, almost as though the house were alive and glaring straight toward Amanda.

CHAPTER 2

Paul Furby flew down the stairs two at a time. "Who's ready to party?" he cried when he landed with a thud at the bottom. Typical Paul. The Peterson girls had known Paul for what seemed like forever. He was in seventh grade with Alyssa at Glory Middle School and towered over all three of the sisters with his tall, wiry frame. Paul was wearing his usual outfit: gray jeans, a plaid flannel shirt unbuttoned over a black T-shirt, and sneakers. He leaped into the center of the room, threw up his hands, and whipped his head to flip the hair out of his eyes. It was Paul Furby's signature move.

Alyssa took one look at Paul and rolled her eyes. He was the first of the Peterson sisters' friends to arrive.

Paul loved being the center of attention and would no doubt have everyone laughing at his corny jokes and goofy dance moves later. But now he only made a mad dash for the jelly beans and started tossing them into the air and catching them with his mouth.

Amanda giggled as she watched him tumble backward while trying to catch an overthrown jelly bean. Someone tapped her on the shoulder, and she turned to find Carrie Hernández grinning back at her. Carrie looked over to Paul and back to Amanda, giving her a knowing look and wider smile.

"You're finally here!" Amanda squealed, giving her friend a quick hug. "What took you so long? It's almost eight." Carrie was actually Alyssa's best friend, but Amanda had known her for so many years that she was almost like a second older sister.

"I couldn't decide what to wear," Carrie replied.

"I've heard that before!" Amanda teased. Amanda looked at her, and as always, Carrie was perfectly dressed. Her jeans and blue velvet top complemented her smooth olive skin. Amanda noticed she was wearing a hint of makeup and knew that Mrs. Hernández sometimes allowed it for special occasions. The green eyeliner

21

made Carrie's eyes glimmer and pop. She was one of the nicest kids at Glory Middle School, and she was friends with everyone. Her outfits always matched her sunny outlook and fun personality. Tonight was no different.

Carrie playfully nudged Amanda, but it was a little too hard since Amanda stumbled and bumped right into Paul. Jelly beans scattered all over the floor. Amanda and Paul dropped to their hands and knees, recklessly scooping up the candy, when she accidentally knocked foreheads with him.

"Ouch!" he shouted, rubbing a spot directly above his forehead. "Are you trying to knock me out?"

"Sorry!" Amanda said, jumping up and hurrying over to where Alyssa's MP3 player was docked. Carrie followed her.

"I didn't mean to push you," Carrie whispered. "I promise!"

Amanda fiddled with the MP3 player. "Don't worry about it. Do you think Paul looks cute tonight?" she asked.

Carrie answered by teasingly batting her long, dark eyelashes. "Amanda," Carrie said. "I think you're blushing."

"I am not," Amanda replied, but she could feel her cheeks burning. "Anyway," Amanda said, trying to compose herself, "I've created a special playlist for tonight." She turned up the volume as Carrie walked over to the basement's makeshift dance floor.

"I hope there's some dance music on there," Olivia Lange called from the basement's bottom step. Amanda rushed over to her and gave her a quick hug. Olivia was carrying a pillow and large overnight bag. Amanda could see several outfits jammed into it.

"I've been waiting for you! Put your things over there," Amanda instructed, pointing to a growing pile of sleeping bags, pillows, and duffel bags. Olivia dug into her giant tote and pulled out a tube of lip gloss, adding a final swipe to her already shiny lips. She stuffed it into her pocket and carelessly threw her bag on top of the pile.

"Do you think you've brought enough clothes?" Amanda asked, teasing her fashionista friend. "You're only staying one night!"

"You never know what you'll need," Olivia replied. "And I like to have an outfit for every emergency situation!"

Amanda giggled, knowing her best friend was only partly joking. Olivia was in sixth grade with Amanda and shared the responsibilities of being cocaptain of the volleyball team. When Olivia wasn't playing volleyball, she was rooting for the boys' football and basketball teams as Glory Middle School's head cheerleader.

Tonight, Olivia's pin-straight, dark brown hair was in a ponytail fixed high on her head. It swished back and forth when she walked.

"I've changed five times already," Olivia told her. Amanda admired her final choice: a red-and-silver sequined cardigan over dark leggings that were tucked into black suede boots with puffy pom-poms on them.

"You're even glowing!" Amanda replied.

"It's magical fairy dust. I may let you borrow some," Olivia whispered, nodding toward the dance floor. Amanda followed her gaze and saw Paul spinning until he couldn't help but stop and then shake his head, trying to regain his balance. He looked so goofy that Amanda and Olivia burst into laughter until they were gasping for air.

"It looks like Paul got a haircut," Olivia finally said. Amanda looked at Paul's sandy blond hair. It was still wavy, disheveled, and almost reached the bridge of his nose. But it did look just a touch more cropped around his ears and the nape of his neck. She knew his mom must've forced him to get it trimmed, because Paul didn't really care about his hair—or anything else about his appearance for that matter. He was too busy trying to make people laugh with his silly antics. Once again Paul flipped the hair out of his eyes so he could see.

"Really?" Amanda replied. "I hadn't noticed." The two girls looked at each other—both knowing that *nothing* about Paul Furby slipped by Amanda—and doubled over with laughter again.

Slowly more guests arrived. The girls' friends were mostly gathered around the food table, picking at the snacks and pouring themselves cupfuls of punch. Carrie was trying her best to get people dancing, pulling them into the center of the dance floor with her, and Alyssa and Amanda stood nearby giggling at her unsuccessful attempts.

"It might take people a little while to warm up," Alyssa reminded her.

"Exactly," Amanda agreed. "Why don't you show them how it's done, Alyssa? Not everyone knows how to pirouette around the dance floor like you do!"

Alyssa was about to protest her sister's teasing when she suddenly heard Amanda make a tiny gasp and followed her gaze to the foot of the stairs. Steve Turner had arrived. Amanda glared at her sister, daring her not to say a word, as her cheeks burned and turned slightly red from embarrassment. Alyssa dramatically shook her head.

"You are so busted!" she told Amanda. "All this time, I've been thinking you had a crush on Paul. It looks like he's been replaced by the new kid."

"What?" Amanda replied, snapping herself back into the moment. "No. I don't like him. I just didn't know you invited him."

"He's in my class," Alyssa replied, still smiling at her sister's shock. "And he's new to Glory. I thought it would be nice for him to become part of our group. Meet new people."

"I think it's a really good idea!" Amanda agreed.

Both sisters watched Steve walk into the party, and even Alyssa had to admit that he looked slick and cool, just like every day at school when he came into her fifth-period algebra class. The Turners were Glory's newest residents—and this was big news since hardly anyone ever moved to or from Glory. This instantly made Steve one of the most popular kids in school, but Alyssa admired him for more than that. He was from Philadelphia, which meant to Alyssa that he was everything that Glory was not. He listened to bands that she had never heard of before and did things that most kids in Glory didn't really care about, like sitting alone and drawing in his notebook. He would rather skateboard in the park than play football. Alyssa had even overheard him telling a group of guys at school one day that he was taking guitar lessons. But mostly, Steve had a way of walking into a room. Without even trying, everyone felt his presence. He could turn heads by just being Steve. His confidence was what Alyssa really liked about him. Admittedly, like her sister, she also didn't mind his messy dark curls and startlingly blue eyes.

Alyssa watched Amanda flush as Steve walked over to them.

"You are so predictable, Amanda," Alyssa whispered. Amanda shrugged and shot her a look, pretending she didn't know what her sister was implying. But they both knew that Amanda had recognized how cute Steve looked tonight. He was wearing washed-out, ripped jeans and a plaid button-down shirt over a long-sleeved T-shirt.

"Hey!" Steve greeted when he reached Alyssa and Amanda. "Alyssa, thanks for the invitation," he continued. "I know my mom and dad are really looking forward to spending time with your parents and some of Glory's other finest tonight!" Amanda laughed loudly at Steve's little joke. Alyssa raised an eyebrow at her sister's obvious flirting.

"We're really glad you came," Alyssa said. "Did you find our house okay? Sometimes people get lost when they first come out here."

"Or think they're lost when they do finally get to our little dirt road!" Amanda added.

"Yeah," Steve replied. "That's actually why I'm so late. We missed your road twice and had to turn around. This is great—it's really off the beaten path, isn't it? You're sort of out here alone."

"Oh, we're used to it by now," Amanda said.

"Though I think my dad was a little nervous while driving, since it's so dark without any streetlamps," he told them. "And my mom was sort of freaked by that old house next door. We accidentally pulled up to it, but then we realized that all the cars were parked here. What's the story with that house?"

Suddenly, Paul was standing next to Steve. They bumped fists in greeting.

"Ah, my man Steve," Paul said. "That's Glory's famous haunted house. The Petersons' only neighbor for miles. Didn't you know?"

CHAPTER 3

Alyssa squirmed. This is exactly what she didn't want to happen. From out of the corner of her eye, she saw Amanda frown. The sisters hated when the house next door came up in conversation. It was a sore spot between the sisters and their friends. Their friends always wanted to tell stories—some passed down through generations—about the strange things they'd heard of happening in that old house. But Alyssa and her sisters didn't want to talk about it at all. *Ever.* It made the mood of any party turn from cheery to eerie. Their friends always got to go home after the frightening tales, but Alyssa, Amanda, and Anne had to look at the house out of their bedroom windows before they went to sleep every night.

"Seriously, you guys?" Anne came over and threw herself into the conversation. "Are you really afraid of some abandoned old house?" Just as Anne said these words, Alyssa's eyes caught Amanda's. All the color seemed to have drained from Amanda's face. She was as pale as a ghost. Alyssa knew it wasn't like Amanda to act like this in front of boys, and she was instantly concerned.

What's wrong with her? Alyssa wondered. Sure, she and her sisters had experienced bizarre things with that house over the years. She would never forget the time, a year and a half ago, when her mom sent her outside to collect basil from the herb garden for the pasta boiling on the stove. Alyssa was terrified. She never really liked being outside by herself—it was just so dark. And the Petersons were isolated, being at the end of the dusty road all by themselves. But to be honest, the real reason she felt so strange about being outside by herself was that she never really felt alone in the slightest. Instead, she always felt like someone was watching and following her every step. Sometimes, the feeling got so intense—like eager eyes were burning a hole into her back—that she would whip around, fully expecting to come face to face with one of her sisters spying on her. But every single time, she would discover that no one was there.

So on this particular night she hesitated before going outside to get basil. She knew she was just being silly—and figured nothing could be worse than her younger sisters knowing that she was actually afraid—so she grabbed a flashlight and took off through the sliding glass door and into the backyard.

She walked just beyond the house to the small garden. It was surrounded by a low fence that kept out the pesky rabbits that liked to nibble on her mom's herbs. Alyssa stepped over the fence, shined the light on the plants, and searched for the leafy basil. As she grabbed a handful of leaves, she felt a pair of eyes watching her. Her back felt exposed to the world. Breathing deeply, Alyssa turned around. Nothing. Her flashlight darted around the darkness. Still nothing. Alyssa exhaled with relief, but she also felt a little ridiculous since, once again, she'd let her fears get the best of her.

Alyssa took another deep inhale, forcing herself to be comfortable in the darkness. But in those few seconds a dim, soft light—maybe a glowing candle—illuminated the spaces between the slats in the shutters of the attic window in the abandoned house. Alyssa froze. She'd never known anyone to be inside the house. Alyssa saw a shadow move in the light and then stop. Could the shadow be a person? And was he or she watching Alyssa?

Alyssa dropped the flashlight and basil, and ran toward the safety of her own house as fast as her feet would go. By the time she reached the kitchen, tears were streaming down her face, and she hysterically told her family what had happened.

"I'm sure it was just a local teenager," Mr. Peterson told Alyssa as Mrs. Peterson held a comforting arm around her. "Nothing to be afraid of."

"Will you please go outside and see for yourself?" Alyssa managed to say through fits of sobs.

Mr. and Mrs. Peterson went out together to investigate. Alyssa eagerly waited for them to come back into the house and tell her what they had found. But her parents only returned with Alyssa's flashlight and the basil. They hadn't seen anything out of the ordinary. And they certainly hadn't seen any light in the neighboring house's window.

"But someone is in there!" Alyssa cried. "I'm not seeing things!"

After much urging, Mr. Peterson called the Glory police station to report what his daughter had witnessed. The sheriff was quick to arrive. Alyssa watched through a window as the police car drove up the road and blue-and-red lights flashed around the old house. After about ten minutes, the cruiser drove over to the Petersons' home.

The sheriff sat at the Petersons' kitchen table and drank a cup of coffee as he told them what he found. As it turned out . . . nothing. The doors were locked. The windows were tightly latched. And there was no sign of any trespassers—no graffiti, no lights, and no evidence at all that someone had been in the house in what the sheriff suspected was many, many years.

From then on, whenever Alyssa felt nervous outside at night, she made herself remember that her eyes could easily play tricks on her.

About a year later, Amanda confided that she believed what Alyssa had seen. One hot night, this past summer, Amanda walked into Alyssa's room and sat down on her bed beside her. The air conditioner wasn't working, and the stickiness was making it hard for Amanda to sleep. At least that's what she told Alyssa at first. What had really kept Amanda awake—and what had been keeping her awake for weeks—was her mind replaying the whispers she'd heard while retrieving her softball that one afternoon.

Amanda hadn't repeated the exact words she had heard whispered to a soul. But on that hot summer night, her sleeplessness finally got to her and the words she had heard finally spilled out. "Stay away," she repeated to Alyssa. In the heat, Alyssa felt the familiar, cold sensation of fear surge through her.

She squeezed Amanda's hand. "Don't worry," she told her. "Let's talk to Anne tomorrow. Maybe she's seen or heard something too. Then we can all go together to talk to Mom and Dad."

The next morning, however, Anne laughed when her sisters confided in her. She mocked and teased them for their foolishness. She boasted that although she was the youngest, she definitely wasn't afraid of some old house.

Alyssa didn't want Amanda to recall these memories, least of all tonight. Alyssa had to bring her sister out of her cloudy daydream before anyone else noticed her ghostly expression and their carefully planned New Year's Eve party turned into a Halloween spook-fest.

She quickly grabbed her sister's elbow and steered her over to the snack table.

"Serve these," she told Amanda, shoving into her sister's hands the plate of beautifully frosted, silver-sprinkled cupcakes Alyssa had baked earlier. Amanda looked at the cupcakes in surprise and then nodded, grabbed the plate, and headed directly over to Paul.

"Cupcake?" she offered to him.

"Don't mind if I do," he replied, plucking two from the plate. "You know," he continued, "when we drove up, my mom said ever since she's lived in Glory that house has been exactly the same."

Alyssa rolled her eyes again. She wished that Paul would just let it go!

"The town tried to put it up for sale a few times," Olivia added.

"It's in shambles," Carrie said. "No wonder why nobody wants to buy it!"

"I heard that some married couple thought about buying it a few years ago," Olivia said. "But when they went inside they heard footsteps, like someone pacing back and forth, on the floor above them. They freaked out and rushed to the front door to leave, but when they reached it, it slammed shut and locked itself. They had to unlock three dead bolts to get the door open. I guess someone, or something, didn't want them to leave."

"That's ridiculous!" Anne jumped in. "These are just stupid, made-up legends about some boring, old house. Nobody in Glory has anything better to talk about."

"That's not what I heard," Paul said. He spoke slowly, in a deeper-than-usual voice. Something about him seemed uncharacteristically serious. "It's true that the town did try to sell the house, but it wasn't to a couple. It was to a single woman. And it definitely didn't work out."

Anne scoffed, not believing her ears—this story was actually a new one. She thought she had heard all the rumors by now.

Paul continued, "The woman had heard people whispering about rattling doors and windows, but she just chalked it up to the house being so old. It didn't bother her at all, not when she could buy the house for such a steal. When she was ready to sign on the dotted line, she stopped by the house for one final visit to snap some pictures to send to her family.

"Slowly, she checked each room. There was nothing suspicious. She made her way to the attic. The small room was once used as a bedroom. It struck her that it must've been a little kid's room because it still contained a tiny neatly made-up bed, a small desk, a single nightstand with a harmonica on it, and some old-timey wooden toys around the floor. She felt a little sad, looking at the room that once belonged to a child, but nothing was out of the ordinary, so she decided that all the rumors about the house being haunted were just that, rumors.

"She turned to leave when she heard a small knock coming from behind an old chest of drawers on the far side of the attic. It was a pattern of knocks, like a code. Tap, tap-tap, tap. Tap, tap-tap, tap." Paul knocked his knuckles against a nearby table, mimicking his words. *Tap, tap-tap, tap.* "Over and over, like someone was there, trying to get her attention. She slowly made her way over to the dresser. It was dark, too dark to see anything. So she flicked on her flashlight, and a beam of light lit up the area. She was shocked by what she saw. . . ."

Paul stood silent in the middle of the room. Several pairs of eyes glared back at him.

"What?" Amanda asked. "What did she see?"

"Nothing," Paul replied.

"You're so annoying, Paul," Alyssa told him.

"All I said was that she didn't see anything in the attic," Paul said defiantly. "But a few days later, on her way to the bank to finish signing the papers for the house, she swung by the drugstore to pick up the pictures she had developed. This was in the olden days before digital cameras were invented. She reviewed the photos of the house while she was still in the store. In each photo, the figure of a girl, a ghost, stood in the background.

"When she reached the end of the pack, she screamed and dropped all the pictures, leaving them on the floor of the drugstore when she ran out. The woman never showed up to the bank to sign the final papers and was never heard from again."

The room was quiet. Alyssa was stunned and speechless.

"No way!" Anne shouted, breaking the silence. "That kind of thing happens all the time! Haven't any of you guys ever seen those ghost hunting shows? They always debunk the ghosts in pictures as being tricks of the light."

"I wouldn't believe the story unless I trusted the person who told me about it," Paul countered. "The woman who developed the photos was my aunt. She thought the same thing about tricky lighting, maybe the person was experimenting or something. But when my aunt saw the woman's face, she knew that the images terrified the woman. My aunt tore up the photos the woman dropped, and threw them away, never wanting to see them again."

"I don't believe it," was all that Alyssa could mutter.

"Neither do I!" Carrie agreed. She looped her arm through Alyssa's. "And besides, who cares about that dumb house? Halloween was two months ago, Paul. We're here tonight to have a rockin' New Year's Eve party. What do you guys want to do next? More dancing?"

Alyssa let out a small sigh of relief. Within a minute, Carrie was practically dragging Steve into the middle of the room, completely ignoring his resistance.

The Peterson sisters remained in a darkened corner of the room, watching their friends dance. Anne was getting into the music and was just about to join their guests on the dance floor when she heard Amanda whisper, "They're just rumors."

Alyssa and Anne turned to look at their sister. She still had a phantomlike complexion.

"Of course they are," Anne told her, and skipped off to the dance floor.

Amanda nodded, willing herself to believe her younger sister. Because after everything that she just heard about the house, there was one thing that she couldn't stop thinking about. *Could it have been the same little girl from the pictures who opened the shutters tonight?*

CHAPTER 4

"Listen up!" Carrie shouted over the music about a few hours later. "It's New Year's Eve and less than two hours till midnight. I think everyone knows what that means!"

Amanda's eyes lit up. She knew exactly what that meant, and she couldn't wait. Amanda had never been kissed. Even though the New Year's kisses at their previous parties were just on the cheek, the boys had always just ignored her. She had been thinking about this night for months now, and she was determined that this was her year to be kissed at midnight!

At this point, everyone was hot from dancing inside, and they had grabbed their jackets and wandered out to the porch to cool off. The sky was filled with clouds blocking out the stars, but the tea lights twinkled in the dark night. Everyone milled around in small groups. Alyssa had brought some of the snacks outside, and the table overflowed with cupcakes, brownies, and the Petersons' famous snack mix. She had even set up a mix-it-yourself fruit juice and soda bar—complete with mini scoops of ice cream and tiny umbrellas. A few of Anne's friends sat in the large wooden Adirondack chairs, sipping punch out of plastic champagne flutes and whispering to one another. Every so often they would point to the huddle of guys and giggle.

Fifth graders, Amanda thought and smiled.

Amanda searched through the crowd until she found Paul. The new kid, Steve, was cute, but she'd had a crush on Paul for forever. He had always treated her like a younger sister, but Amanda wasn't a little kid anymore.

"We should start thinking about who we'd like to kiss when the clock strikes twelve!" Carrie finished her announcement.

At the mention of being kissed, the fifth-grade girls squealed with delight. Anne's best friend, Jenna Lee, covered her eyes as her cheeks burned bright red. Carrie clapped excitedly while the boys let out groans in shock and horror. Daniel Garrity plunged an imaginary dagger into his heart and then dropped to the floor. And Matt Weber pretended to puke uncontrollably.

"You're all so immature!" Carrie chided.

The more the girls tried to hold it together, the harder it was not to crack. When Steve started blowing kisses and batting his eyelashes at a squirrel that ran across the yard, everyone finally broke into a fit of hysterical giggles.

While everyone was distracted, Amanda grabbed a box of sparklers from the table and pulled out two of them. She touched the end of one to a nearby candle's flame, and it burst into a shower of sparks. It lit up her face and cast a pretty glow around her. She walked over to Paul and held the unlit sparkler out to him.

But Paul's attention was far away. He was staring across the yard and out into the darkness. Amanda could tell that he didn't even know that she was standing next to him.

Suddenly, Paul pointed toward the old neighboring house. Amanda followed his gaze. The house was barely visible. A thick blanket of clouds hid the moon. She simply saw a dark silhouette against the backdrop of the night. She glanced back at Paul and watched his expression.

Paul was sort of smiling, deep in thought, but then all of a sudden he frowned.

"What?" Amanda asked.

"Did you see that?" Paul whispered. "A light flickered in the top window."

Amanda turned toward the house, but it all looked dark.

"I don't see anything," she replied.

Paul didn't seem to be paying attention. He was still looking into the night, distracted. "Someone is inside that house," he said.

Again, Amanda looked across the field. The old house remained as dark and lifeless as ever. For an instant, she thought that Paul was pulling her leg, playing one of his famous practical jokes on her. She was about to call him on it when she saw a flash of alarm in his eyes. Amanda panicked, seeing that Paul was seriously freaked. What exactly did he see?

"So who are you going to kiss at midnight?" she asked, desperately trying to change the subject. She nudged his arm and handed him the unlit sparkler. He absentmindedly took it from her. Amanda leaned in to light it with her own sparkler, but it was too late. The one she had been holding fizzled out with a final hiss and a slowly rising wisp of smoke.

Paul ignored her question. Amanda was about to urge him to rejoin the group when Anne walked over. He didn't even notice her standing beside him on his other side.

"I want to know what's going on in that house," he continued. "Someone's in there—playing with the electricity or candlelight or something."

"That house is spooky. We get it!" Anne cried. "It's just your eyes playing tricks on you. It's probably a camera flash bouncing off the windows from our parents taking pictures upstairs."

Paul now looked at Anne. He lifted his head and puffed his chest a little. "Yeah, of course," he said. "I wasn't scared or anything."

"So, you agree?" Anne asked. "Everything people say about that house is just plain silly?"

"We totally agree!" Amanda said, answering for the both of them while shooting her little sister a secret smile. "Besides, I think Alyssa has some games planned. Let's go back to the group."

The corner of Paul's mouth lifted slightly. He flipped his hair and nodded.

Amanda found Alyssa refilling the bowl of pretzels.

"We need a game to distract everyone. *Pronto!*" Amanda told her.

Alyssa looked at her, but she didn't ask any questions. She disappeared inside for a minute, and came back onto the porch with a dusty, old hat filled with folded slips of papers. Earlier that day, Anne and Alyssa had spent a good hour coming up with the craziest things their friends would have to act out for a game of Charades. They thought of everything from scuba diving to some of their favorite movies. They wrote each prompt down on tiny strips of paper, and put them into the hat. They even had a prize for the winner: a plastic gold trophy they found at the dollar store.

"Who's up for a game of Charades?" Alyssa asked. A large circle of kids had gathered around her.

"Great idea!" Carrie cheered.

Steve agreed. "I'll go first."

"I don't think so," Alyssa cut in. "We need to pick teams."

Olivia's eyes crinkled as a mischievous smile spread

across her face. She had an idea. "Girls against boys?"

"Perfect," Paul agreed. "Prepare to be defeated." He pulled a quarter out of his pocket and balanced it on his thumb. "Heads or tails?"

"Heads!" Carrie, Anne, and Amanda called out together.

Paul flicked the coin into the air, and everyone took one step back as it plunked down in the center of the circle. The girls groaned. Tails.

"Steve," Paul announced. "You're up." He bent down to pick up the quarter and then shoved it back into his pocket.

Alyssa lifted the hat high enough so that Steve could pick out a piece of paper without seeing what was written on it. But instead of reaching his hand into the hat, he grabbed it away from Alyssa.

"Hey, where'd you get this old hat?" he asked.

"Give it back, Steve," Alyssa said. "You're ruining the game."

"It's really cool," Steve replied. Alyssa tried to grab it, but Steve was too fast. They were tugging the hat back and forth until finally Steve let go and Alyssa faltered backward. As she tried to regain her balance, she let go of the old hat, and it fell to the ground, spilling and revealing the prompts. Alyssa looked at them scattered around on the porch, and her cheeks grew red with embarrassment.

"Are you happy now?" Alyssa asked.

Steve looked sheepish as he bent over and started collecting the paper slips. "Sorry," he said. "You're not mad at me, are you?"

Amanda jumped in. "It's okay," she told him. "Anyone have another game?"

"I do," Paul blurted out.

"What is it?" Amanda asked, desperate to move attention away from her sister, knowing that Alyssa would die of embarrassment if any of her friends saw her so upset.

"Truth or Dare," Paul said.

Amanda glanced at Alyssa to see what her older sister thought of Paul's suggestion. Alyssa nodded. They'd all played Truth or Dare a million times in the past—what was the worst that could happen?

"Okay," Amanda agreed. "But nothing crazy."

"Crazy?" Paul replied. "Me? Do something crazy?" He stood silent for a minute. "Who will be the first victim?"

He clasped his hands behind his back and slowly walked up to each of the guests. One by one, he bent down and peered into his or her eyes, and then he stood up and moved on to the next person. Nervous giggles followed him around the porch.

Amanda held her breath, hoping Paul wouldn't choose her. She didn't want to pick Truth. What if Paul asked her who she liked? And she definitely didn't want to have to choose one of his crazy dares.

When Paul reached Steve, he stopped and pointed. Steve pretended to be shocked that Paul chose him. "Steve," Paul began, "truth or dare?"

"Easy," Steve replied. "Dare."

"I dare you," Paul continued, "to sit in that abandoned house for ten minutes. Alone. In total darkness.

CHAPTER 5

"No. Way," Alyssa said sternly. "No one is going to set foot off this porch. My parents would be so angry!"

"Yeah," Steve agreed.

Paul tilted his head in Steve's direction. His eyes crinkled as the corner of his mouth lifted into a lopsided grin.

"It sounds like you're scared, Steve," Paul said, ignoring Alyssa. "Are you too chicken to accept my dare?"

Steve ran fingers through his dark, wavy hair. "I didn't say that," he said good-naturedly.

Alyssa stood as straight as she could muster—pulling her shoulders in just like she had been taught in dance class—in an attempt to look taller than she really was. She looked back and forth between the two boys. "Nobody is going anywhere," she said. "And that's that."

Amanda watched her sister start to lose her temper. Alyssa looked more upset than she'd ever seen her before. Amanda had to act fast—the thought of the boys disregarding Alyssa and going inside the old house alone in the dark, filled her with dread.

She grabbed Alyssa's elbow and steered her away from the table. "Just a sec," she told their friends. "We'll be right back."

As soon as they were out of earshot, Alyssa looked extremely worried. "What are we going to do?" she whispered with the intensity of a yell. "We're not allowed to get too close to the house. Remember what Mom and Dad told us? We're responsible for our friends during the party. We have to do something!"

Amanda took a deep breath and put one of her hands on her head. She looked over at their friends. "I know," she replied, remembering their parents' warning.

Alyssa lowered her voice a few octaves and mimicked their father's sing-song southern twang. "If you're old enough to host your own New Year's Eve party, then you're old enough to keep the party in line."

Amanda smiled, and she also mocked their dad. "Don't let your mother and me down." She wagged a finger at Amanda. "And don't you forget it!"

"We have to get everyone back inside," Alyssa replied. "The outdoor portion of our party is over. Follow my lead."

Alyssa immediately started blowing out the candles that glowed around the porch, hoping everyone would get the hint that it was time to head back in. Amanda followed, blowing out a few more tea lights on the opposite side of the porch. "Game over," she told the group. The light filling the porch dimmed with each extinguished flame. It was almost pitch black, except for the inside lights that cast a faint glow over the porch.

"But we've hardly started," Paul complained.

"I don't think anyone really wants to play Truth or Dare anyway," countered Alyssa.

Paul sighed and walked over to the wooden box where Amanda kept some of her sports gear. He picked up her basketball and then balanced it on his middle finger. He gave it a swift spin. Amanda watched it spiral round and round. Steve and Matt walked over, and started chatting with Paul, who kept the ball twirling. A few years ago, Paul tried to teach Amanda how to do the trick, but she never got the hang of it.

Just then a jagged bolt of lightning splintered through the sky, illuminating the fields around them. The lightning's glow cast wiry shadows of tree branches onto the fields. An ear-shattering crack followed, barely muffling the high-pitched shriek that filled the air.

"Whoa!" Steve said, looking up at the sky. "Lightning. A thunderstorm in winter. I'm still not used to that."

Alyssa nodded absentmindedly. While her friends were staring at the light show in the sky, she searched for the person who had let out that scream. She quickly spotted Jenna slumped down in a wooden chair with her knees pulled up against her chest and her arms wrapped tightly around them. Anne had squatted down on the arm of the chair next to her. Alyssa rushed over to them. She knew that Jenna could sometimes be a little dramatic, but Alyssa could see that Jenna's trembling was real. Jenna pulled her cardigan around her legs, like she was trying to become invisible or protect herself from something.

"Jenna?" Alyssa asked. "What's wrong?"

"That house," Jenna replied, pointing a finger into the darkness. "The door. It just flew wide open!"

Alyssa strained her eyes, trying to peer through the darkness. But without another flash of lightning, it was no use. She couldn't make out the house.

"Are you sure, Jenna?" Anne asked, grabbing her friend's hand. "That house has been locked up tight for years—maybe it was just a trick of the light?"

"No," Jenna replied, standing up and talking a little too loudly. "You know better than anyone that strange things go on at that house. You told me. Your sisters think that the house next door is haunted!" Everyone turned around as she said these words. And then it was silent. All that could be heard was the hollow *thump, thump, thump*ing of Paul's dropped basketball, bouncing on the porch floor.

"Haunted?" Paul asked, pushing his hair out of his eyes. "So the rumors are true. Why did you deny it earlier?"

"Because it's not haunted," Alyssa said defensively. "It's just an old house. Decaying and decrepit, nothing more."

"Come on," Steve countered. "Don't keep the truth a secret. I didn't grow up here like you guys. Remember? Fill me in!"

And that's when a light bulb went off in Alyssa's head. If the guests at the party wanted ghost stories, she could give them ghost stories—just as long as they didn't involve that stupid house.

"This whole thing just gave me an idea," she told the group. "Who wants to tell scary stories?" She looked pleadingly at Carrie, hoping she would agree.

"I've got about a hundred famous Glory ghost stories!" Carrie added.

"Excellent," Paul said. He turned to pound fists with Steve.

Alyssa smiled at her friend. Finally, something was going the way she wanted it to. She locked arms with Carrie as they began to walk toward the sliding glass doors. Carrie smiled back and looked from Alyssa to Amanda conspiratorially. "This could be a good idea," she said to Amanda. "There's nothing like being scared half to death to make you feel like grabbing on to someone." She gave Amanda a knowing look.

"W-what?" Amanda stammered. She felt her cheeks burn.

"You know, you could grab on to Paul," Carrie suggested in a whisper. "Everyone knows you like him."

Alyssa giggled as Amanda scoffed. Alyssa walked to the door and slid it open. "Let's go," she told the guests. "Everybody, inside."

Their friends left the porch and followed Amanda and Anne into the house. Alyssa hung back and looked around at the clutter her friends had left behind.

"I'll be right in," she announced to the crowd. "I'm just going to quickly clean up out here."

The night had been fairly warm, but the impending storm was ushering in a chill. Alyssa hugged herself and thought about just leaving the mess for the morning. She didn't want to miss any of the fun, but she changed her mind when she considered her parents finding the mess before the girls were able to clean up. This was their chance to impress them—to show that they could be trusted with their own party.

So, with a heavy sigh, Alyssa started to collect the plastic cups and cupcake wrappers that had been thrown on the ground. She was just about finished when she noticed the tray of veggies and ranch dip turned completely upside down on the table. Grabbing a handful of napkins, she wiped up the sticky pools of goop and threw them into a trash bag. Alyssa took a final look around for any stray cups or hidden veggies that she may have missed.

Suddenly, the fields around the house were illuminated again. Another series of lightning flashes streaked across the sky, and three shattering claps of thunder followed. Alyssa jumped, her heart beating triple time. She concentrated on tying together the trash bag with clumsy, trembling hands. Her head jerked up when she heard pounding. She looked around, not knowing if she was confusing the sound with thunder or if it were something else entirely. The pounding continued. She spun around, wanting to search for the source of the noise, but also afraid of what she might find in the darkness. Her eyes fell upon the old house across the fields. Another lightning burst pierced the sky, and Alyssa watched the front door swing open and close. Open and close, pounding heavily and angrily against the doorjamb.

Dropping the trash bag, Alyssa ran inside. Her heart thumped in her chest. She closed the sliding glass door behind her and locked it, yanking it twice to make sure it was secure. From inside the safety of her basement, she stared in the direction of the old house, waiting for lightning to illuminate the sky and the fields, but all remained dark.

"I'm going crazy," she mumbled to herself. She rubbed her eyes and turned her back to the glass doors.

"Alyssa! We're almost ready," Carrie called.

Alyssa glanced back over her shoulder just once before joining her friends. She saw nothing but her reflection in the glass.

On the other side of the room, Anne cut the music and dimmed the lights. There were a few nervous giggles as everyone's eyes adjusted to the darkness. Amanda grabbed a flashlight from the utility cupboard and handed it to Carrie. Alyssa crouched down next to her best friend.

"Give us your best shot," Alyssa whispered to Carrie. "Just please no stories about the house next door."

"You got it," Carrie agreed.

Alyssa darted her eyes around the room, straining them in the darkness, to make sure all their guests were accounted for and no one had gone back outside. She found Amanda sitting next to Paul and Steve, and she sat down near them. She held her breath so she wouldn't giggle when she saw Paul whispering to Amanda.

"Don't worry," Paul told Amanda. "I'm here if you get scared." Amanda tried not to notice that they were sitting so close their knees touched.

"All right," said Steve loudly. "Please, please, please, please can we hear just a little bit more about the house next door? Everyone is clearly spooked by it."

"Just one story wouldn't hurt," Anne added. "I've got some. I've been over there tons of times—"

"No, you haven't," Alyssa interrupted.

"At least I'm not scared of it!" Anne replied defensively.

Amanda clenched her jaw and glowered at Anne. Anne looked back innocently, pretending not to be hurt by her older sister's scowl.

"Now you *have* to tell us!" Steve continued. His mouth curled into a grin.

"Okay, just one story about the house," Amanda told Carrie.

"Amanda!" Alyssa scolded.

"I don't know," Carrie said hesitantly. "I guess just one couldn't hurt? Then we can just drop the whole thing." She looked at Alyssa. Alyssa let out a big sigh and reluctantly nodded.

Steve and Paul high-fived each other. They'd won. Carrie would tell the story everyone wanted to hear.

"It's a good one," Carrie began, "but it's not really a ghost story. It's a true story—a very spooky true story."

Alyssa turned to her sister with a raised eyebrow. She watched Amanda silently mouth a single word: *Relax!* Alyssa rolled her eyes and turned her attention back to Carrie.

"Like most everyone here, I was born and raised in Glory," Carrie began. "And so were my parents. But unlike a lot of people living here today, my grandparents and even great-grandparents were born here too. There have been Hernándezes living in this town since it was founded more than one hundred years ago. We're like Glory royalty."

Carrie's audience was captivated. *She has a way of owning a room,* Alyssa thought.

"My family knows everything that is anything about this town," Carrie said. "According to my grandfather, that spooky house next door was the very first house built in Glory. Before then, this area had just been a military outpost with a few stores and cemeteries—"

"That's not so weird," Anne interrupted.

Carrie went on. "The house was really monumental for its time. A young family traveled here from back east and built it themselves. The mother and father had three small children. Their last name was Goodwin. After a couple of years, other settlers followed, and they built houses a few miles away. One of those families was mine. Pretty soon, a little town had sprung up, and everyone was calling it Glory. My great-grandmother met the Goodwins several times. She told her son, my grandfather, that they were always polite and kind when they were in town, but they mostly kept to themselves and spent *a lot* of time working on the house—fixing it up and renovating small sections of it.

"The house always had a lot of bizarre problems. And as soon as Mr. Goodwin would fix something, it would break again. It took all the family's time and energy to keep it in order. . . . It was almost like the house never wanted them to leave. To the other townspeople, it looked like the Goodwins had become obsessed with making it perfect, but the more they tried, the more things went wrong with the house. Then, one year, a few days after the new year, people in Glory began to notice that they hadn't seen the Goodwins in a while. When they went out to the house to check on them, the Goodwins were nowhere to be found. The family had simply disappeared without a trace."

The room was dead silent.

"Rumors spread like wildfire," Carrie told them. "Some people said that the family had simply left one night, but others believed that something more sinister happened. That the house was evil. That it had trapped them inside, but then why couldn't anyone see them? Perhaps the house was somehow haunted and that the demons that lived there lured people in to trap them. Some even believed that the house fed on the people."

Everyone hung on Carrie's words. "Of course, these are just rumors."

A few of the guests exhaled in relief. Amanda realized she'd been holding her shoulders tensed up toward her ears. She let them relax and fall.

"But," Carrie continued, "don't forget that the house has been abandoned ever since—for one hundred years. And my grandparents and their friends have always believed that someone—or something—has occupied it.

Strange things have happened around that house, just ask Elena."

Alyssa slumped. She peered out of the corner of her eyes and saw all her friends turn toward Elena Sandhu, waiting expectantly for her to tell them what she knew about the house. Alyssa noticed two of Anne's friends clutching each other so closely that they were practically sitting on each other's laps. She knew that the kids at the party—especially the younger ones—were starting to get scared. She couldn't see little Jenna in the crowd, but she was hoping that she wasn't too shocked. Alyssa jumped up, ready to turn the lights back on.

"It's true," replied Elena.

Sighing, Alyssa sat back down on the floor. Her efforts to avoid this story would be useless.

"So what exactly has happened at that house?" Anne asked pointedly.

Elena shifted uncomfortably. She had a habit of tugging her sleeves over her hands when she was nervous. And now everyone could sense that her nerves were on edge.

Sensible Elena, who had spoken in front of the entire

school as student-body president of Glory Middle School, was shaken.

"I don't really like talking about it," Elena admitted. No one had ever heard her speak so softly.

"Maybe it's time to stop," suggested Alyssa.

"No. I'd like to tell it," said Elena. "It's a story about my grandmom. She grew up in Glory too, as you all know. If you get her started, she'll talk for hours about how great Glory was back in the day. She goes on and on about how everybody knew everybody. People never locked their doors. You could really depend on your neighbors—that sort of thing. She would play in the streets without a care in the world. Glory has always been a bit sheltered from the rest of the world—especially back then—when everyone looked out for one another.

"But if you've met my grandmom, you know that she's not exactly . . . friendly. She's always been the strict one in our family. According to my great-uncle, she didn't used to be that way. He says that I remind him of her when she was young, but something happened to her that changed her. She built a wall around herself and stopped trusting people.

"He only told me the story of what happened once. And when I asked my grandmom about it, she just stared at me coldly and touched her bony finger to my heart. It was the only time I ever saw her hand tremble. And then she told me never to ask her about it again."

"What was it?" Anne asked. "What happened to her? What did your great-uncle tell you?"

"Great-Uncle Walt said that my grandmom's best friend when she was a girl was a boy who lived down the street. His name was John. They did everything together. If he went fishing, so did she. They would take long walks and pretend to be explorers discovering a foreign land. One day, on one of their adventures, they stumbled upon the old Goodwin house."

Elena turned and looked at each of the Peterson girls. "Your house hadn't been built yet," she said, and then she went on. "My grandmom refused to go inside. Her parents had always forbidden it. John teased her and went inside alone while she stayed outside on the lookout. My grandmom was so happy when he came back out a few minutes later."

"So what's the big deal?" one of the boys in the back called out.

Elena looked down. "The big deal is that he must have loved exploring that house and went back a few more times without her. And then, one day, he and his brother just disappeared."

"What does that have to do with the house?" Amanda asked.

"Great-Uncle Walt told me that my grandmom is convinced to this very day that something happened in that house. Something that caused her very best friend in the world to vanish forever, and she thinks that maybe, after all these years, he and his brother might still be in there."

"I don't believe in ghost stories," Anne whispered.

"Well, I don't either," replied Elena. "But the look in my grandmom's eyes that time I asked her about it convinced me that she was scared of something. And it scared me, too."

Elena was finished speaking, but no one said anything to fill the silence.

Suddenly a slow, drawn-out screech—much like fingernails being dragged across a chalkboard—broke the silence. Alyssa noticed a change in the room's temperature, as if the air conditioner had been turned on full blast. Next to her, Elena shivered in the cool air.

Alyssa jumped up to turn on the lights. Her fingers fumbled along the wall until she found the switch and flicked it on.

In the light, Alyssa gasped in horror.

There were two large gaps in the room were Paul and Steve had been sitting, and the sliding glass door stood wide open.

They were gone.

CHAPTER 6

Anne jumped up and ran to the sliding door. Amanda followed her. They peered out into the darkness, but they couldn't see anything beyond the porch. Paul and Steve were definitely not within their range of vision.

"Where are Paul and Steve?" Carrie shrieked. "Amanda, Paul was sitting right next to you!"

"I know," she replied. "I guess I got so wrapped up in Elena's story that I didn't notice them sneak away. I don't know where they went!"

Amanda suddenly felt very guilty. Her friends had disappeared, and they had been sitting right next to her.

"I know where they went," Alyssa said slowly.

"They went to the house next door."

"Try their cell phones," suggested Carrie. "Maybe you can convince them to come back before they go in there."

Alyssa picked up the cordless house phone and dialed Paul's number. She heard a faint buzzing sound coming from a pile of jackets on the couch. When she felt the pocket of Paul's jacket vibrate, she turned the phone off and looked at her friends.

"Try Steve's," suggested Amanda.

Once again, Alyssa made a call from the phone. When she heard a familiar jingle of chimes also coming from the pile of jackets, she hung up, feeling defeated. Paul and Steve were gone, and they hadn't even bothered to bring their phones.

"Even though the game of Truth or Dare is over, Steve must have accepted Paul's dare," said Carrie.

"This is crazy," Alyssa told Amanda. "We specifically told them not to go over there."

"Paul's probably loving that they will scare us by sneaking off," Amanda added.

The three sisters exchanged a quick worried glance and then looked away, trying to shake off their fear.

Anne, Alyssa, and Amanda were sensible. They weren't expecting any creatures of the dark to swoop in and hurt Paul and Steve—they were more concerned about the boys walking through an abandoned house at night. There were bound to be loose boards and rusty nails that couldn't easily be spotted in the dark. At least that's what their parents told them time and time again. And that's just what they would say tonight if they found out the boys had left the house.

The house *was* dangerous. After all, it was more than one hundred years old and had been left to rot for most of those years. If Mr. and Mrs. Peterson found out that two of the girls' friends went over there this late at night, it would be the last New Year's Eve party hosted by the Peterson sisters.

"Someone's got to go and get them," said Carrie.

"I will," Anne volunteered. After all, she was definitely the bravest of the three sisters. Everyone knew that.

But she was also the youngest, and Alyssa shook her head. Anne was not going over to the house.

"Why not?" Anne demanded. "I'm the only one here who's never been afraid of that house. If anyone goes, it should be me."

Alyssa grabbed Anne by the sleeve and guided her away from their friends. She admired Anne's fearlessness, but Anne was just too young to wander into the night by herself. Alyssa was determined that her little sister would stay safely inside.

"Anne," Alyssa said. "We need you to stay here with our guests. Make sure nobody else leaves this basement. Think of a game or something to take everyone's mind off of the scary stories. Can you do that?"

Anne crossed her arms and huffed. This was a classic Alyssa move. She was always reminding Anne that she was too young. Once again, she would be left behind while Alyssa had all the fun. Anne had been looking for an excuse to explore that house for ages, and this was her chance. It just wasn't fair.

Amanda hurried over to her sisters. Her forehead was wrinkled with worry.

"We really have to get going if we're going to find Paul and Steve!" Amanda said urgently. "It's almost eleven. What if their parents want to leave right after midnight?"

"And who is this 'we'? Where do you think you're going?" Alyssa asked her.

"I'm going with you," Amanda replied. "There's no way you're going over there alone!"

"You're not going," Alyssa said firmly. "Stay here with Anne."

Amanda looked her older sister directly in the eyes and shook her head. "You can't always boss us around, Alyssa," she continued. "It's better that we both go."

Alyssa looked from Anne to Amanda and then out the sliding doors behind them. It was so dark beyond the porch, and she finally admitted to herself that she didn't really want to go alone.

"All right," Alyssa agreed, and she and Amanda headed over to the sliding glass door.

Anne followed them. "Shouldn't you bring a flashlight or something?"

"Oh, good idea," Alyssa said.

Amanda walked over to the cabinet that their mom always kept filled with outdoor supplies: bug spray, citronella candles, batteries, etc. She grabbed two flashlights, flicked them on to make sure they worked, and handed one to Alyssa. Amanda shot Alyssa a look.

"What's the plan?" Carrie asked.

Alyssa took a deep breath and looked at her friends.

"Amanda and I are going outside," she replied. "Everyone else stay here with Anne."

"You're going out into the dark?" Elena asked.

"Yes," Alyssa said. "We need to go out, and maybe even into that old house, to find Paul and Steve. And then we're going to bring them back here and *kill* them!"

Anne laughed under her breath, though she knew her distraught sister was only half joking. She certainly didn't want to be Steve or Paul when Alyssa finally found them.

CHAPTER 7

Alyssa and Amanda stepped off of the security of their back porch and into the black night. They switched on their flashlights and scanned the field for any signs of Paul and Steve. The grass was motionless. Alyssa and Amanda darted their flashlights in all directions. Not a movement. Not a sound. Alyssa followed her sister's gaze to the second floor window of their own home. The faint glow reminded Alyssa that their parents would soon ring in the New Year. And then it would time for everyone to leave.

"We have to hurry," Amanda said. "And, as much as I hate to admit it, I think we should turn off our flashlights until we reach the house." She knew her sister was nervous outside in the dark, but she also didn't want any of the adults to spot the beams of their flashlights from the upstairs windows.

Alyssa nodded and grabbed her sister's hand. Slowly, they each took a step toward the house next door. Without their flashlights, Alyssa and Amanda shuffled along an old beaten, cobbled pathway that led to the meadow. Fallen leaves squished under their feet with each step.

As they continued in the direction of the silhouetted house, both sisters suddenly stopped dead in their tracks. The grass and branches rustled behind them.

"Did you hear that?" Alyssa asked Amanda urgently.

They spun around to see stalks of grass shaking and quivering in front of them. Something was following them. Alyssa was paralyzed with fear. But, Amanda took a step forward to investigate. Steadily, Amanda switched her flashlight back on and focused the beam of light on the moving grass. There was definitely something in there. Step by step, she moved closer. When she reached the rustling grass, she leaned forward to get a better view. The flashlight trembled in her hand.

"Be careful!" Alyssa whispered.

"I know!" Amanda replied. She crouched down and parted the grass with her hands. Accompanied by a loud, piercing *caw*, a large shiny black wing skimmed her face. Amanda screamed just as loudly as the crow and fell backward onto the ground. The crow sprung from its hiding spot on the ground and flapped its way upward, taking flight into the night sky. Amanda let out another terrified wail, followed by a whimper.

"It was just a bird," Alyssa told her, sitting beside her in the grass. The two sisters were silent, hoping that no one at the adult party had heard the scream. Then Alyssa noticed Amanda's bloody fingers, which were tightly holding the flashlight. Amanda flashed the light on her hand and then the stinging area on her leg to reveal a small scrape. She must have gotten the scrape when she fell backward and then her hand brushed against it. A fine line of blood trickled from the wound and down into her shoe.

Alyssa hated the sight of blood. She felt her stomach turn over. Feeling queasy, she positioned herself into a squat and put her head between her knees. She forced herself to take a few deep breaths and waited for the nausea to pass.

"What happened?" she asked Amanda. "Why are you bleeding?"

"I think I stepped on a twig. It must've snapped and scraped my leg," Amanda explained.

"Do you want to keep going?" Alyssa asked hopefully. Now the idea of going there on her own made her feel dizzy too.

"No big deal." Amanda pulled her sleeve over her hand, and wiped the dirt and blood from her leg, applying pressure to her scraped skin to stop the bleeding. When it had stopped, she stood up and brushed the muck and leaves from her skirt. "Let's go."

The girls continued through the meadow, flashlights off. With each careful, soft step they moved closer to the house. It was a deafeningly silent night, and the only sound the girls heard was the swishing of grass brushing against their legs. But, along with each rustling footstep, they could hear hushed voices. Warnings.

Neither girl said anything until Alyssa finally squealed and turned angrily toward Amanda.

"Why did you pinch me?" Alyssa asked.

"Because I can hear you whispering," Amanda replied. "You're freaking me out!"

"I haven't said anything!" Alyssa exclaimed.

"What do you mean?" Amanda asked. "I heard you say, 'Stay away!'"

"Amanda," Alyssa replied, "it wasn't me. But I heard it too."

"Well," Amanda continued, "if it wasn't you, then who was it?"

The girls stopped. They had made it too far to turn around now. Alyssa switched on her flashlight and frantically swung the beam around. The beams only showed the emptiness that surrounded them though. They were completely alone.

"I think we should head home," Amanda told her sister. "We can just fess up to our parents, and they can deal with Paul and Steve." Alyssa hesitated for a second. She also wanted to return, and Amanda's idea wasn't a bad one, but why should their parents' party be ruined too and their parents' trust in them be shattered because of Paul and Steve?

"The voices we're hearing are just Paul and Steve playing a trick on us," Alyssa replied reluctantly. "Come on. The sooner we find them, the sooner we can go home."

They continued walking, turning their flashlights on periodically to scan the area ahead for Paul and Steve. Every so often, Alyssa would call out each boy's name. But she didn't receive any response. They only heard the quiet whispers drifting through the still night. They squeezed each other's hands with each passing warning. They were both trying to convince themselves it was simply their minds playing tricks on them, scaring themselves witless. That the stress of the situation was getting to them. But how could they both be hearing the same thing?

They stopped when they finally reached the steps leading up to the house's front porch. For all the years they lived next door, this was actually the closest they had ever been to it. And now that they were so close, they took a moment to examine all its eccentricities. The house was sturdier than Alyssa expected—she always thought the wooden shingles looked flimsy, but now that she was so near them, she could see the walls beneath the shingles were thick and solid. The paint had long since cracked and had been worn down by years of stormy weather and hot summer days. Rusty nails poked through the sagging floorboards of the porch.

Amanda was about to take a step forward when Alyssa squeezed her hand and jerked her back. Even though the thick walls of the house and solid oak door supported the house's foundation, the porch hadn't held up as well. The wood planks were rotting and decayed.

"Follow me," Alyssa instructed. "You're going to go right through if you're not careful!"

Alyssa let go of Amanda's hand and placed her foot on the first step. And, with the poise and practice of a ballet dancer, she swiftly leaped to the top, gingerly stepping on each stair along the way.

"Now, walk in my steps," Alyssa told Amanda. "And hold on to the handrail."

Amanda looked warily at her sister.

"I don't think I can do that!" she replied. "But don't move. I'll try."

Amanda put some weight on the first step, and just as she had expected, a loud cracking sound shot through the air. Amanda grabbed hold of the iron handrail and tried the second step. It creaked beneath her foot, but supported her. She followed in her sister's footsteps until she also reached the top. Together, they walked toward the door. Suddenly, Amanda felt cobwebs on her arms and hands. She had walked through a giant spider web. Panicking, she began peeling the strands of the web away from her face and arms. "They're all over me!" she screamed. No matter how much she tried, she couldn't seem to wipe all the strands of web from her.

"Stop it!" Alyssa demanded. She was standing before the heavy front door. She studied the ornately carved detail in the wood. There were engraved designs and sketched pictures of birds, rabbits, and other wildlife. But there was also something that looked like a word or name carved into the wood. She traced it with her finger. It looked like someone had scratched it away, and she couldn't make out what it had once said. She placed her hand on the brass doorknob, expecting to have to shove the solid door open, but to her surprise, it was already ajar. *Paul and Steve,* she thought. With a slight nudge, it swung open. Amanda had finally managed to free herself from the web, and, together, Amanda and Alyssa walked through the door and into the house.

As soon as Alyssa entered the foyer her cheeks burned with anger.

"What are you doing here?" she demanded.

Paul and Steve stood before them, illuminated in

the beams of their flashlights.

"Come on," Paul said. "Don't be mad! We just wanted to check out the house. It's awesome, isn't it?"

For a moment, Alyssa was too curious to yell at the boys. Instead, she looked around at the foyer. It was filled with unfamiliar trinkets from many years ago. Large, tarnished bells hung on the wall. She quickly figured that they were once used on a horse's harness before someone had turned them into a decoration. An old box, hanging on the opposite wall, displayed a collection of pewter spoons. And she spotted what looked like old brass or copper buttons on the foyer table. Pushing a feeling of dread out of her mind, she tried to focus on Paul and Steve.

It was hard though because the house fascinated her—it was like she had stepped into a museum. They were all standing in a large square alcove that opened up into a living room with a few old, dusty armchairs and tables. Alyssa walked over to a soot-covered fireplace in the far corner. She peeked around that corner and into an adjacent room. It had to be the kitchen, judging from the dusty, outdated appliances she saw as she moved the beam of her flashlight around the room.

A large staircase was to the left, winding up to the floor above them. Old moth-eaten rugs covered the floors. Faded black-and-white-toned photographs sat framed on the tables.

Alyssa scanned the relics in the room until she stopped at the tall, ticking grandfather clock. It was by far the most stately piece of furniture in the room. Alyssa tilted her head and looked at it pointedly. It seemed to bring life into the otherwise lifeless house. Watching the small hand go around, she thought how remarkable it was that the old thing still worked after all these years. And then she noticed the time.

"It's eleven fifteen!" Alyssa announced. "We have to leave *now!*"

Alyssa turned to leave with Amanda on her heels. Amanda caught Paul's eye. "It's really not cool that you left. If our parents find out that we're here, we'll be grounded forever. If we're grounded, you two are going down with us."

"Relax," Paul replied. "No one will ever know we were gone."

"Famous last words," replied Alyssa.

"It's cool," Steve said, turning to Paul. "This old

house is spooky-looking, but it's actually kind of boring."

Alyssa relaxed for the first time since she'd left the safety of her own party. Everyone was finally on the same page. It was time to go. They headed for the door.

"Hey." They heard an unfamiliar voice calling from behind them. "Leaving so soon?"

CHAPTER 8

All four kids spun around in shock. Alyssa's heart was pounding so forcefully that she felt like it could drop out of her chest and right down into her stomach.

Two boys about their age stood before them. Alyssa and Amanda had never seen them before. They seemed to have just . . . appeared.

"You look like you've seen a ghost," the taller boy said to Alyssa with a smirk. He walked over, extending his hand for a shake.

Alyssa quickly shook his hand.

It was warm. Not ghostly at all.

She could feel her face begin to regain its color. Despite herself, she blushed.

"We're really sorry," the boy said. "We didn't mean to scare you! I'm John."

"And I'm his brother, Michael," the other boy introduced himself.

John was about an inch taller than Amanda. Amanda quickly looked him over from head to toe, hoping he didn't catch her doing so. Her first thought was how neatly he was dressed. His blond hair was perfectly combed, not a strand out of place. His button-down shirt looked crisply ironed and was tucked into his dark jeans that he had rolled up to show his shiny, black penny loafers. Michael, on the other hand, had the same precisely coiffed hair, but it was dark. He was wearing a clean white T-shirt tucked into his dark jeans and similar shiny shoes. Alyssa couldn't help but notice how different they looked from Paul and Steve, who were wearing their sloppy, faded jeans, flannel shirts, and dirty, old sneakers.

Alyssa introduced herself and Amanda to John and Michael. She gave Paul a little push. He got her hint and introduced himself and Steve. Paul, the tallest of the boys, stood straight as a board, showing every inch of his height. He crossed his arms over his chest and began interrogating John and Michael.

"You guys from around here?" Paul asked.

"Nah, we're just visiting," Michael explained. "I'm glad we don't live here. This town is so boring. No offense."

Paul winced. He had complained about how there was nothing to do in Glory plenty of times, but he'd never heard it put so bluntly by strangers.

John stepped forward in an attempt to cover up for his brother.

"We thought we'd take the afternoon to explore," he said. "I guess we got carried away."

"Who are you visiting?" Steve asked.

"Our aunt," Michael replied. "She lives about a mile from here. We're here over the school break."

"What's her name?" asked Paul. "I know just about everyone in this town."

"I don't think you'd know our aunt," John replied quickly. "She pretty much keeps to herself."

"How come we've never seen you around before?" Paul asked.

"This is our first time in Glory," John explained.

Amanda was getting annoyed with Paul and Steve.

"What's with the twenty questions?" she asked. "I'm sorry about my friends. They're used to being the only good-looking guys in town."

Michael smiled at her.

As soon as she realized what she had blurted out, Amanda thought that she might actually melt into the floor. She looked around, trying to find an escape from the four sets of guys' eyes that turned on her.

"Amanda!" Alyssa said. "Check this out!"

Alyssa grabbed her sister's sleeve and walked toward a table, pointing to a small, dusty stained-glass lamp. She turned around to see Paul and Steve still giving John and Michael the third degree.

"What was that?" Alyssa asked. She had pulled her sister so awkwardly that Amanda nearly stumbled over her own feet.

"I don't know!" Amanda replied. "It just came out." Placing her hand on the grimy lamp, Amanda pretended to be admiring it. She dragged her finger along the glass shade, leaving a clean squiggly line in the dust.

"That's gross," Alyssa told her.

When Amanda didn't reply, Alyssa continued, "All

right. It's time to get Paul and Steve and leave. We've got to get back to our party."

"But what about John and Michael?" Amanda asked.

"What about them?" Alyssa replied. "They seem nice, but we really don't have time to get to know them. We have to get back before midnight. Before anyone notices we're gone!"

"That's still like forty minutes away," Amanda said. "Let's just hang out for a few minutes with John and Michael, and get to know them. Maybe they'll want to come back to our house to hang out. We need to play it cool."

"Have you forgotten that we're not allowed in this house?" Alyssa reminded her sister. And then she realized what was going on. Amanda thought John and Michael were cute! Alyssa frowned. "Come on, Amanda. Not now."

"Please, let's just stay a few minutes longer," she begged.

But Alyssa only shook her head. From the moment she had decided to come here to find Paul and Steve, the memory of the shadow that she'd seen in the attic window years earlier was tugging at her.

She didn't want to spend an extra second in this house.

Alyssa took her sister's hand and led her back to where the boys were still talking. Amanda pouted. Now that she was in the house, she didn't really find it spooky at all.

Her sister was being totally unreasonable.

As the girls neared the four boys, they heard Paul and Steve still grilling John and Michael.

"So, have you been here all afternoon?" Paul asked.

"We have," said John. "We didn't even realize how late it had gotten until you reminded us it was almost midnight. What a way to spend New Year's Eve."

Amanda immediately perked up. The boys had admitted to being in the house since that afternoon.

Of course! The slamming of the door. The flickering of lights.

It had been John and Michael! She felt incredibly childish for being so easily spooked. Now all she had to do was convince Alyssa of the same. Maybe her older sister would let them stay.

"Paul said he saw lights flickering in this house earlier," Amanda said. "Was that you? And did you also open the front door? We thought the house was haunted!"

Amanda noticed that John and Michael shot each other a pointed look, but then they burst out laughing.

Michael held up his flashlight. "You must have seen us going through the house using these," he explained.

"Do you believe in haunted houses?" John teased.

Amanda turned to Alyssa. "I guess not!" Amanda said. "Alyssa, do you believe in haunted houses?"

John playfully nudged Alyssa's arm. "You're not afraid of this old house, are you?" he asked her.

Alyssa looked down at her feet as she felt her face burn. "No," she replied. "Of course not."

"Good," he said. "So you won't mind coming with us for a tour." And then he grabbed Alyssa's hand.

Alyssa's cheeks turned bright red, but not from embarrassment. It was more from excitement. She relaxed and looked at her sister.

"Okay," she replied. "But let's do it fast. We have a party waiting for us at home!"

"All right!" John said.

"This way," said Michael.

Alyssa, Amanda, Paul, and Steve followed John

and Michael through each room of the house.

In the small kitchen that sat off of the living room, old pots and pans hung from an iron rack fixed to the ceiling. A nearby china cabinet housed dainty plates and cups.

"At least the rumors were true," Amanda said, looking at the corroded cutlery.

"What rumors?" John quickly asked.

"That nothing has changed about this house in the past century," she replied.

"Let's go upstairs," Michael suggested.

They walked through a room lined with shelves that were filled with tattered books. Amanda picked one up and blew the dust from the cover. Alyssa sneezed, and Amanda quickly placed the book back on the shelf.

The sisters trailed behind the four boys up the wooden stairs to the second floor. Amanda hung to the banister tightly, just in case the stairs were as rickety as the porch steps. She really didn't want to crash through them. At the landing, they all followed John and Michael down a very narrow hallway.

The first room they went into was a bedroom. The

solid four-poster bed that sat in the middle of the room, accompanied by nightstands on each side of it, reminded Alyssa of the one in her parents' bedroom—but this bed smelled like mildew.

An old, open wardrobe displayed dresses that hung from rusty hangers. Most of them were made out of thick, heavy fabric. Their skirts hit the floor and their collars were stiff and high. Alyssa twitched when she saw how drastically the waistlines had been tucked in and wondered how anyone could actually wear something like that. Some of them were adorned with lace, but it had been yellowed through years of accumulating filth and grime. The dresses also smelled awful, like vinegar.

They then went into a second bedroom. A once-colorful knitted blanket was folded over the side of a crib and a set of children's books sat on a table next to a rocking chair.

When Alyssa spotted the wardrobe filled with small clothing, a chill went down her spine. She very carefully picked up a petite jumper, which was something that may have belonged to a child of about two to three years old. She searched through more of the clothes to discover some dresses, too, that may have fit a girl of about six or seven. Returning the clothes to their place, she gave the room one last glance and pictured a woman rocking a baby in the chair. She started to leave but then stopped so abruptly that Amanda, walking close behind, bumped into her.

"What's wrong?" Amanda asked.

"I thought I saw that chair move," Alyssa replied. "Like someone was rocking in it."

Amanda glanced at the chair, but it wasn't moving. She pushed Alyssa down the hallway and walked to the next room. It was a tiny bathroom. A porcelain bathtub that sat on ornate claw-feet almost filled the entire room.

Amanda grimaced, thinking about having to soak in a bathtub instead of taking a long, hot shower.

They moved along to the very end of the hallway and turned a small, sharp corner.

By the time Alyssa and Amanda arrived, the boys had already ascended the little staircase that led to the attic.

Alyssa shuddered. This was the moment of truth. She was finally heading up to the attic where she had seen the shadow many months ago.

"I can't go up there," she told Amanda.

"I know it's creepy," Amanda replied. "But it's creepier staying down here by yourself."

Alyssa exhaled, gathering her courage, and nodded. She let Amanda slip by her to lead the way, and they both climbed the steps to the attic. When Alyssa arrived, she saw the boys crammed in the tiny room. The ceiling was so low that Paul had to bend down so he wouldn't bump his head.

"It's insane," Paul said. "Right?"

Alyssa was speechless. She glanced at Amanda, also not able to find the words to explain how she felt. Everything about the attic was how Paul had described it earlier.

It was exactly what his aunt saw in the pictures many, many years ago—down to the bed, the desk, and the harmonica on the table.

"Paul," Alyssa said, "you tricked us."

"I've never been here," Paul pleaded, but Alyssa just glared at him.

It was at that moment that a slamming sound came

up from the basement. Alyssa reached for Amanda and clung to her tightly. No one moved—frozen by fear—as they listened to the thunderous crash of hundreds of objects being shattered below.

CHAPTER 9

"What was that?" Steve shrieked. Alyssa had never heard one of her guy friends sound so scared. He spun around, swiveling his head in every direction. He pointed rapidly to the floor with a shaking finger. "There's something down there!"

Alyssa's heart jumped in her chest. It sounded like glass had been broken. But now it was silent. With wide eyes, she looked from Paul and Steve to John and Michael.

"This is getting way too weird for me!" Paul said nervously. "I'm out of here."

Paul flew down the attic steps with the crew chasing him down the hallway. When he reached the second staircase, he took the steps two at a time until he landed at the bottom. Alyssa was breathing deeply from exertion and fright when she caught up to everyone in the foyer.

"Wait," John said. "This is an old house. It was probably just something that fell over."

But Steve's hand was already on the doorknob.

"You're both leaving?" Amanda asked. Confused, she looked to Paul and then back to Steve.

Paul pushed past her, making his way out of the living room. But when he reached the foyer, the rubber sole of his shoe snagged the corner of an old, tattered rug. He tried to steady himself, but he tripped over his feet and started to tumble toward the floor. As he reached out to break his fall, he grabbed on to a grimy cloth that covered a small table. The tablecloth slid off the table, causing all its contents to come crashing to the floor.

Amanda walked over to where Paul was sprawled out on the rug. The springs and cogs of a small broken clock were scattered about the floor. A vase had shattered. And several yellow-tinged papers floated about until gently settling around him.

"Are you okay?" Amanda asked, stifling a laugh. The sight of Paul grappling on the floor made her completely forget just how spooked she had been only a few seconds earlier.

He looked at her with bloodshot eyes. Amanda wondered if he was about to cry.

Amanda and Alyssa couldn't believe what they were seeing. Paul and Steve were scared. Alyssa bit her bottom lip and tilted her head.

"Everyone else leaving too?" Steve asked.

"Actually," John spoke up, "I think we're going to stay. Who knows what other neat things might be hidden in this house? Maybe there's a secret passageway that leads to a hidden treasure. Why don't you stay?"

"No way," Steve replied. He pulled on the solid oak door until it finally opened. "See ya!" he called as he ran out of the house. He jumped off the porch, leaping over the wobbly step.

Alyssa went to the door and watched him sprint toward her home. She blinked and he disappeared into the darkness.

Paul scrambled to his feet and brushed the dust

off of his jeans. He left big, gray handprints on his backside.

"I'm still gonna head back too," he said. Little glass pieces crunched under his feet as he made his way to the door. As soon as he hit the ground outside, he also raced off into the night, slipping away into the shadows.

Alyssa looked at Amanda, and they both broke into a fit of hysterical laughter. Amanda was nearly shrieking as she gasped for air.

"Tough guys," John quipped.

"Yeah," Amanda agreed. "And they were so excited to get here earlier."

After they calmed down, Alyssa remembered the loud crash that came from the floor beneath them. "What do you think crashed when we were in the attic?"

John looked at the girls and smiled. "I guess there's only one way to find out. Let's go see."

As the four kids walked through the living room, and the hilarity of the last few moments faded away, Alyssa began to feel uneasy again. She felt like she was being watched.

She swiveled her head, expecting to see someone

lurking in the shadows or behind the curtains. Of course there was no one there. She was alone with her sister and her new friends. But the feeling wouldn't go away—the sensation of eyes following her every move grew stronger.

"You know what? I really do think it's time to leave," she said as they approached the basement door. "We're having a party. John and Michael, you could come with us. You probably noticed our house earlier today. It's right next door. It's the *only* other house on this road."

"We can't leave yet," John said. "We need to make sure nothing is broken in the basement. Maybe something fell over."

"Why?" Alyssa wondered. "This isn't your house."

"Yeah, but what if someone finds out we were here?" John replied. "We don't want to be blamed for everything that's been broken in this house."

He smiled at Alyssa and then looked down and shuffled his shoes.

Alyssa sighed.

She wasn't entirely sure she agreed with his logic, but she returned his smile.

"Come on," Michael urged. "We'll all go down and check it out together."

Alyssa opened her mouth to protest, but Amanda jumped in before she could utter a word. Now that Paul and Steve were gone, she saw a new opportunity for a midnight kiss.

"Just one minute?" Amanda asked.

She looked at her sister, pleading with her not to ruin anything.

"Okay," Alyssa agreed. "But let's make it fast."

The four kids walked toward the basement door in pairs: John walked next to Alyssa while Michael walked closely beside Amanda. When they reached the door, John opened it and led the sisters down a narrow wooden stairway.

The basement smelled dank and stale. The four kids swung their flashlights around, illuminating the dark room.

Alyssa and Amanda looked around with wide eyes. If being in the upstairs rooms of this house wasn't creepy enough, the basement took it to a whole other level.

It was stuffed with relics. Amanda peered at the shelves and shelves of old toys that lined the walls—broken tin cars with dented and scraped exteriors; clown figurines dressed in faded, torn silk costumes were missing limbs; and a large tarnished music box with a tiny dancer in a black tutu that remained open but had long-since been silenced.

Blankets of dust covered an antique wooden wheelchair and steel chest. An ancient player piano had been shoved into a corner.

But what really made Amanda's skin crawl were the rows and rows of jars.

She walked along the shelf, peering into each one. They were filled with all sorts of things—from nails and bolts to thread and needles. Someone had used them for storage.

She stopped in front of one jar that appeared to be filled with . . . eyeballs. Lots and lots of tiny, round eyeballs.

"Doll's eyes," John offered, walking up behind her. "We spotted them earlier."

Amanda simply looked at him and then continued examining the jars. When she approached one that was filled with a gooey, flesh-colored liquid, she stopped again, waiting for John to explain this one.

"I don't know," he admitted. "Maybe some sort of jam? Or canned food?"

"Alyssa," Amanda whispered. "Look at all of this stuff. It all must've belonged to the family that lived here—the ones that vanished. If they had moved away all those years ago, why would they have left this stuff here?"

Alyssa picked up a large handmade teddy bear that was coming apart; its stuffing was peeking out at the seams. An eyeball hung off it's face. The thread holding it seemed like it could break at any moment.

"I don't know," she replied. "Somebody must have loved these things at one time. Now they just sit here collecting dust."

A small rustling sound jolted Amanda to attention, causing the hairs on her arms to stand on end.

"Did you hear that?" she asked. Alyssa nodded skeptically.

The rustling grew louder, loud enough to pinpoint where it was coming from. There was something moving behind the steel chest.

Alyssa stared fiercely at Amanda.

"I told you we should've gone back with Paul and

Steve!" she whispered harshly.

Suddenly, Alyssa screamed. She grabbed Amanda's hand, digging her nails into her sister's skin.

A small black fur-covered paw darted out from behind the steel chest. It ran its claws along the floor and then scurried back behind the chest and out of view. Amanda made a small step toward the chest.

"Amanda!" Alyssa said sternly. "Do not go near that chest."

Amanda stood frozen. "What should we do?" she asked.

"We should leave," Alyssa replied.

"Why, because you're scared?" John asked. He walked over to the chest.

"Be careful," Alyssa warned.

John peeked over the chest and reached his arm behind it. Suddenly, he dropped to the floor. He began to rapidly convulse and pull on his arm, but it was stuck. Something was attacking it from behind the chest!

Alyssa screamed again.

John broke out into fits of laughter, then he calmly stood up.

"Sorry," he said. "It was just a joke!" He motioned for Alyssa and Amanda to join him. "It's okay," he told them. "I promise. You can trust me."

Amanda cautiously walked over to where John was standing.

She peered behind the chest and gasped. A small black cat, wearing a red leather collar, was dashing back-and-forth while playfully pouncing on a crumbled ball of newspaper.

"It's just a cat!" Amanda squealed. She had never been so pleased to see a cat in her life. She bent down to stroke its fur, and it purred in delight.

Alyssa lightened up and joined her sister in petting the animal and scratching under its chin. Amanda began to tease it, tossing the newspaper and watching it rush to attack it, when Alyssa remembered how infuriated she was with John and Michael. They were really starting to get under her skin.

She stood up and looked them in the eyes. "That wasn't funny!" she told them.

"It was sort of funny," Michael replied. Amanda was about to argue back when she heard a small whimpering echo coming from the darkest corner of the basement.

The whimpering turned into full sobs. It sounded like . . . a child. Amanda gazed at the corner. Her curiosity overcame her, and she slowly began to walk in the direction of the soft sobs.

"Who's there?" she demanded.

CHAPTER 10

A head of dirty-blond hair emerged from the hollow corner. A girl with dirt swiped across her face crawled into the light.

"Anne!" shouted Alyssa. "What on earth are you doing here?"

Her sister shook as she cried.

"I wanted want to play a prank on you," Anne explained. Her face was streaked with tears. "A prank for leaving me behind. I'm always getting left behind. I decided to sneak into the house."

"You followed us?" Alyssa asked. "How did you get in here?"

Anne nodded her head. "I went through the basement

door, so you wouldn't see me behind you. But it was so dark down here. And then I saw glowing eyes!"

"It was just the cat, Anne!" Alyssa told her.

"I didn't know that! I tried to leave, and I got spooked!" she explained. "I ran back to the door, but it slammed shut and I couldn't get out. I pulled and pulled, but it was stuck."

Anne crumbled into a heap on the floor. She was cold and terrified.

"You must have been so scared," Alyssa said, kneeling down and wrapping her arms around her youngest sister.

After all these years of admitting Anne was the bravest sister, Alyssa couldn't help but wonder how a little cat had positively petrified her.

"I was not!" Anne blurted out between tearful sobs. Alyssa looked at her youngest sister. "Okay, yeah," Anne admitted. "I was scared. Really scared."

Alyssa brushed a few stray strands of hair away from her little sister's face.

"I hid when I heard you coming down the stairs," Anne continued. "I didn't want you to see me so afraid of an old basement."

"Anyone would be scared," Alyssa said. "We heard the door slam, but I'm sure it was just the wind that did it. There's really nothing to be afraid of in this house. It's just old and abandoned is all. No ghosts here."

"I didn't feel so brave," Anne replied.

"Not brave?" Alyssa asked, exaggerating her surprise. "I would never have come over here by myself. Never mind in the dark! You're braver than anyone I know, Anne."

They sat silently for a moment. Anne had stopped crying and her previously short, jagged breaths were now calm and slow.

Alyssa stood, and she and Amanda helped Anne to her feet.

"Meet our new friends," Alyssa told Anne.

"I'm John."

"And I'm Michael."

Both boys shook Anne's hand. Anne noticed how polite they were—much nicer than the kids she knew from school.

"This is our youngest sister, Anne," Alyssa told the boys. She was relieved to see Anne manage a smile.

Alyssa was also glad Anne was starting to feel better,

but she wasn't entirely sure that her words of reassurance were true.

Alyssa thought back to the loud crash that had followed the slamming of the door. She looked around to see what could have caused such a racket. Although there were an overwhelming number of items in the basement, the knickknacks and pieces of furniture were somewhat neatly organized, as if someone had taken great care to keep them placed as they had been all those years ago.

That was when Alyssa spied the objects that must have fallen and caused the crash.

She walked to the far side of the room and saw that an entire shelf of large, lifelike porcelain dolls had fallen to the ground.

She reached down and picked one up. A jagged crack ran along the doll's face.

Alyssa looked deeper to examine the damage. Maybe the dolls could be fixed. Maybe she could even bring them back to her mom. They might be worth something.

As she brought it closer, the doll's closed lids sprung open; its pupils rolled back and forth in its porcelain head.

Shocked, Alyssa dropped it and the doll shattered into a thousand pieces among the others. She watched as the tiny shards bounced and finally settled.

Then, all at once, ten sets of tiny eyes from broken porcelain faces popped open and stared back at her.

CHAPTER 11

Alyssa's scream this time was so piercing that Amanda's hands went instinctively to cover her ears.

Then Anne began to wail. "I want to leave now!"

"What happened?" Amanda asked, rushing over to her fear-stricken older sister.

"The eyes!" Alyssa shrieked. "They were closed! Then they opened all by themselves!" She was finding it difficult to find the words to explain what had happened.

Amanda bent down to inspect the shattered dolls. She carefully picked up a doll's head and watched its eyes roll back and forth and its eyelids open and close.

John and Michael walked over.

"They're just dolls," John told Alyssa. "The force of the door slamming probably knocked the shelf loose." He pointed to the basement door.

Surprisingly, it was now wide open and let in a draft of cool air.

"I pried it open earlier," Michael explained. "While you were playing with the cat."

Alyssa sighed in relief. A small gust of wind must have gently forced the dolls' eyes open. She took Anne by the hand and guided her through the racks of old clothes and ancient objects toward the stairs.

When she reached the foot of the stairs, Alyssa turned around to take a final look at the sleek black cat before heading upstairs, but instead of seeing the furry animal pawing its way about the rubbish, another object captured her attention. Fresh fear filled her veins. The old wooden wheelchair that had remained still in the room for the entire time they had been down there was now moving back and forth, ever so slightly. She looked at the open door and decided a small breeze must be causing it to sway.

Alyssa turned around and climbed the stairs after her sisters. When she reached the family room, Amanda noticed Alyssa's still-ghost-like complexion.

"Honestly, Alyssa," Amanda said to her when she entered the living room, "you look like you've just gone through Paul Furby's haunted Halloween house!"

"It's okay," John assured her. "Blinking doll eyes would scare me too! But I think we all know that the wind is to blame—that's really all there is to it."

"Of course," Amanda agreed. "Everything can be logically explained. You're just scaring yourself."

Alyssa nodded.

"Well, I guess I should head back," said Anne. "Everyone coming with?"

"We're having fun," Amanda told her youngest sister. "Stay with us for a while."

"I don't know," Anne began. "I'm still a little creeped out from earlier."

"We wouldn't let anything happen to you," John assured her.

"Right," Michael agreed. "As long as you're inside, you'll be safe forever."

Anne looked at the boys and wondered if they were flirting. She suddenly realized why boy-crazy Amanda wanted to stay. John and Michael were totally cute!

"Actually, we should leave now," Alyssa told her sisters. "We're cutting it too close to midnight. If we stay here much longer, Mom and Dad will absolutely notice we're gone."

But instead of immediately agreeing with her older sister, Anne wandered into the foyer, marveling at all the old things, just as her sisters had done earlier.

"Okay," Anne told Amanda, ignoring her oldest sister completely. "I'll hang out for just a little while."

"Perfect!" Amanda almost squealed.

Alyssa looked like she might pull them both out of the house, but then she softened her expression. "Okay, but as soon as the clock strikes midnight, we're out of here."

"What should we do?" Amanda asked. She glanced at the grandfather clock. There were only five more minutes till midnight. Midnight, she reminded herself. Midnight could mean a kiss. A flurry of butterflies flitted in her belly.

"Well," John said, "since Anne was hiding earlier and we found her, maybe we should play an official game of Hide-and-Seek? Just a quick round to pass the time until midnight. And then we'll all leave."

"You girls hide," Michael suggested. "John and I will find you."

John and Michael turned their backs on the girls and started to count backward from one hundred.

With stifled giggles the sisters whispered to one another that they should separate, making it a real challenge for the boys to find them. They scrambled off to find their hiding places.

As soon as the girls were off, the boys turned around just in the nick of time to see the direction each sister had headed.

Amanda and Alyssa both headed for the kitchen. Amanda opened the door to a large pantry. There was just enough room for her to squeeze inside. She sneezed as she closed the door behind her and heard a sharp "Shh!" from Alyssa, who was crouched underneath the kitchen table.

Each minute lasted as long as a lifetime for the girls hiding. They were giddy with the anticipation of having the boys spring on them, discovering their hiding spots.

When they could no longer hear the boys counting, Alyssa popped her head out to get Amanda's attention, and whispered to her. "Doesn't it seem like we've been waiting a long time?" she asked.

"They're probably still looking," Amanda replied. "Let's wait just a minute longer."

Amanda rubbed her eyes and started to feel tired for the first time tonight. But her thoughts went back to counting down till midnight . . . and the kiss that would come when John or Michael found her.

In the foyer, John and Michael had stopped counting. They had waited a few minutes and then stood directly in front of the tall, antique grandfather clock. They watched as the second hand ticked its way toward the twelve. When the first chime rang out, John mouthed, *Go!* and the two boys sprinted through the front door.

"We can't just leave all three of them," Michael said, once they had jumped down off the porch. "There's no need. I think we should at least go back for Anne. She's only a little kid." He ran back inside, just as the clock chimed for the third time, and ran upstairs to find Anne hiding underneath the four-poster bed in the master bedroom.

"Found you!" Michael said. "Hurry, let's go outside.

I think I saw your sisters leaving through the front door!"

Anne followed Michael through the door and onto the porch. John carefully hopped down the steps and onto the ground. The seventh chime rang.

"Here," Michael said, offering her his hand. "Let me help you." Anne grabbed his hand and followed him down the rickety steps. As soon as she reached the ground, John and Michael playfully teased that they had found her first.

"Under the bed was the first place anyone would look!" John said. "You should've seen the look on your face!" Anne doubled over with laughter. She squealed with delight as the boys joked with her.

She was laughing so hard she barely noticed the ring of the twelfth bell. It was midnight. The new year was here.

"All right, time to find my sisters," Anne said.

Michael and John suddenly stopped laughing. A look of fright passed over their faces. Anne looked at them quizzically—they seemed very serious. She walked to the side of the house to look for Alyssa and Amanda. The boys ran to her.

"Wait!" Michael exclaimed. "It's good luck to kiss someone at midnight."

John and Michael each kissed Anne on a cheek. Then they ran off.

Anne stood in place, stunned. The boys jumped up and down, cheerfully hooting and hollering while they ran quickly away from the house. She suddenly felt vulnerable standing outside all by herself.

"Alyssa!" Anne called. "Amanda!"

Back inside, Alyssa and Amanda also heard the clock chiming, announcing midnight. They emerged from their hiding places and stood silently until the clock bells stopped. Alyssa knitted her eyebrows together.

"Why didn't John and Michael try to find us?" she asked.

"I don't know," Amanda replied disappointedly. Another New Year's Eve had gone by. Another year without receiving a kiss. "Let's find them."

Room by room, they searched. They looked behind every sofa and chair, and underneath each table and bed. Finally, they realized they were alone in the house. No John. No Michael. And no Anne.

"I guess we should just go home," Amanda suggested.

"No way!" Alyssa replied. "We definitely can't leave without Anne."

"She must have already left," Amanda offered. "We'll look outside for her. If we can't find her, we'll go home. We can always come back for her."

Alyssa couldn't imagine her youngest sister leaving without them, but what other choice did she have? She opened the heavy wooden door and looked out past the old porch. She was still unnerved by the dark and quiet, and she grabbed Amanda's hand for comfort.

They each took a step past the threshold of the house out onto the porch and into the night.

A split second later, Alyssa and Amanda were standing—once again—*inside* the house, looking out onto the porch.

"Huh?" Amanda asked. She looked at Alyssa, begging for an answer. Alyssa looked stunned and horror-stricken. She let go of Amanda's hand and shook her head.

"We've been in this house too long," Alyssa panicked. "I'm starting to lose it. Let's go!"

The sisters walked past the threshold of the door

again, and once again they were instantly transported right back inside the house. Amanda felt a cold, slick layer of sweat on her skin. She was starting to panic.

"Alyssa!" Amanda screamed. "Why can't we leave?"

"You try this time," Alyssa told her. "Alone. I'll stay in here."

Amanda walked through the door and was immediately transported right back next to her older sister.

"What happened?" Amanda asked.

"Nothing," Alyssa replied. "It was like you never left my side."

Again and again the sisters tried to walk through the house's threshold, into the outside world. Each time they were left staring out into the night from *inside* the house.

Alyssa's heart pounded. She didn't know how it had happened, but she knew what it meant. "We're trapped!" she screamed.

Alyssa pulled her sister by the hand into the kitchen. She opened the back door and walked through it. Again, within the blink of an eye, she was whisked back inside the house. Alyssa ran down the basement stairs with Amanda on her heels. The door that had been wide open earlier was now securely shut. Alyssa tried to open it, but it wouldn't budge. Using all her might, she finally pried open the door.

"Go through it," she said.

Amanda took a deep breath, closed her eyes, and walked through the door. When she opened them, she was standing directly in the same spot. That's when Amanda started to cry. "We're stuck in this house!"

CHAPTER 12

Alyssa wrapped her arms around her shaking sister. She was also freaked out and trembling, but she tried her best to remain calm for Amanda. No matter what, she was the oldest, and she knew Amanda would need her now more than ever. She replayed the events of what had just happened over and over. How could they be trapped inside this house? She steered Amanda back upstairs.

"We can't quit trying," she told Amanda. "Let's try every door and every window. There has to be a way out!"

"Let's stay together no matter what," Amanda replied, taking in gulps of air.

"Of course. We'll try the kitchen door again," Alyssa

replied calmly. But the same thing occurred each time they attempted to leave the house.

They traveled from room to room, wildly searching for a way out. Each time they failed. Defeated, Amanda made her way back into the living room and dropped onto the old sofa.

"We haven't tried a window yet," Alyssa said. "Just wait here. I'll go through it."

Alyssa opened a window and tried to climb out. But just as she expected, as soon as her foot hit the ground, it wasn't the soft grassy earth beneath her feet, but the house's hardwood floor.

Amanda was still making little sobbing sounds as Alyssa continued to pace around the living room. Near the front of the room she noticed a small white envelope on the table with the stained-glass lamp. Had it been there the entire night? How had she missed it earlier? Scooping it up, she stared at the neat block letters that read: **TO THE REPLACEMENTS.**

Alyssa ripped open the envelope to find a folded sheet of lined paper with a note written in the same block letters. She scanned its contents and trembled. Then, she walked over to her sister and read the letter aloud.

DEAR REPLACEMENTS,

IF YOU ARE READING THIS THEN YOU
PROBABLY KNOW NOW THAT YOU ARE UNABLE
TO LEAVE THE HOUSE. THE SAME THING
HAPPENED TO US FIFTY YEARS AGO. AND, FOR
FIFTY YEARS, WE'VE BEEN TRAPPED INSIDE
THIS HOUSE. UNTIL TONIGHT.

IT IS USELESS TO TRY TO ESCAPE. THE
HOUSE IS CURSED. IT NOT ONLY TRAPS YOU
INSIDE, BUT YOU HAVE BECOME INVISIBLE TO
REGULAR PEOPLE. IT'S NOT ALL BAD. YOU WILL
NEVER GROW A YEAR OLDER. AND YOU WILL
NEVER LOOK ANY DIFFERENT THAN YOU DO
RIGHT NOW AS YOU READ THIS LETTER.

IF YOU ARE PATIENT, YOU WILL HAVE YOUR
CHANCE TO LEAVE TOO.

THE ONLY NIGHT YOU WILL BECOME VISIBLE
TO PEOPLE THAT LIVE OUTSIDE OF THIS
HOUSE WILL BE ON NEW YEAR'S EVE . . .

IN FIFTY YEARS. THEN IT WILL BE YOUR TURN
TO FIND YOUR REPLACEMENTS. IF YOU
CHOOSE, YOU WILL BE ABLE TO EXCHANGE
YOUR SPOT IN THE HOUSE WITH TWO NEW
PEOPLE. YOUR REPLACEMENTS MUST BE
INSIDE THE HOUSE AT THE TWELFTH STROKE
OF MIDNIGHT ON THE GRANDFATHER CLOCK
THAT TICKS IN THIS ROOM. YOU MUST BE
OUTSIDE. THOSE ARE THE RULES.

WE ARE SO SORRY TO HAVE DONE WHAT WE
DID TO YOU. SOMEDAY WE HOPE YOU'LL
UNDERSTAND WHY WE DID IT.

JOHN AND MICHAEL

Amanda jumped off the couch in anger. "Is this their
sick idea of a joke?" she shouted. "I've heard of all sorts
of crazy magicians. This has to be a trick!"

Now it was Alyssa's turn to slump down onto the
sofa. She continued to stare at the letter. Then, she felt
that overwhelming and now familiar sense that someone was watching her. She lifted her eyes from the page.

Her gaze drifted over to the large archway leading into the foyer.

A small girl stood before her. The small black cat weaved between her legs.

Alyssa could barely move. She tried to speak, but she could not form any words.

"Who are you?" Amanda asked in a trembling voice.

"I'm Charlotte," the small child answered. "Charlotte Goodwin." She reached out to grab the hand of the man who had suddenly appeared next to her. Beside him was a small boy and a woman holding a baby. They looked like they had come straight out of the old photographs on the nearby table.

The woman swayed and cooed at the baby, lightly patting its back. She smiled at Alyssa. To her surprise, Alyssa felt strangely comforted. "Welcome," the woman said.

"Is it true what this note says? That we can't leave?" Alyssa asked.

"This all must be very confusing for you," the man said. He spoke with a hint of a Texas twang, but Alyssa had never heard an accent exactly like his.

"We built this house over a hundred years ago," he

continued. "We tried to make it the perfect home. And over time it was perfect. But whenever we would go out, something would go wrong with the house. A door would fall off its hinges, or the roof would leak. It got to the point where if we even set one foot out the door, something would collapse inside the house. It became clear that the house didn't ever want us to leave. So we didn't. We preserved enough food so we would hardly ever have to leave. We spent all our time in our perfect house. Then one day, not long after the new year exactly one hundred years ago, a letter was pushed under our front door, informing us of a mandatory meeting in the newly built town hall for all of Glory's residents. We dressed to go into town. But when we stepped over the threshold, we were instantly transported back inside the house, looking out into the vast meadows. Just like you, the house would not let us leave."

"But how can a house do that?" Amanda asked.

"It's not the house so much as the land it was built on. We were as surprised and saddened as you are now," Mrs. Goodwin replied. "We searched and searched until we found an answer. And it was hidden right before our very eyes. We found the original deed from the bank.

In fine print, was a paragraph explaining that the land was historic and sacred . . . and cursed. If we built a house here, we were also responsible for the upkeep of the land. Of course we didn't realize that the land also had certain supernatural elements that would require us to stay here forever."

"But what can *we* do?" moaned Alyssa. "We can't stay here forever! We can't even stay here overnight."

Mrs. Goodwin looked at the sisters with sympathy. She nodded, understanding. "This is our home," she explained. "We are happy to stay here as a family forever. It turned out that the curse was actually a blessing for us, but that doesn't have to be your fate."

"John and Michael had the misfortune of wandering into the house fifty years ago on New Year's Eve," Mr. Goodwin continued. "When the clock struck twelve, the curse was triggered, and they were trapped here with us just as you are now.

"But John and Michael were not happy with their situation. They tried everything to get out of the house. They even tried to burn it down once, but the house found a way to extinguish itself. Then, maybe thirty years ago, the bank hired a psychic. The townspeople must not have wanted to tear down the house since it was the first house built in Glory, but they didn't want it to be abandoned either. They wanted someone to buy it, but no one would, not until the rumors that it was haunted were squashed. Surprisingly, we were able to communicate with this psychic. And she was able to sense things about the curse—things we never could have known. We all listened, including John and Michael, as she explained about the curse taking hold every fifty years. And she explained about the loophole with replacements. Then all John and Michael had to do was wait for their turn to escape.

"Like them, you will have just one opportunity to escape the curse—in fifty years on New Year's Eve— but only if you find replacements. Once the house has claimed more souls, the number of souls has to remain the same.

"We tried to warn you. We knew the boys planned to find replacements. Did you hear us calling out to you tonight? Telling you to stay away?"

"We tried to contact you in other ways," Mrs. Goodwin added. "To scare you even, so you'd run from the house. The dolls' eyes blinking open. The rocking chair and wheelchair. We wanted to do more; to appear and simply tell you to leave." She looked regretfully at the girls. "The house's power is strong. All of our more substantial attempts at communication were blocked."

Amanda and Alyssa nodded, taking in and trying to believe all that they had heard.

Suddenly, the front door swung open. Anne ran inside. Carrie was right behind her. They pointed their flashlights into each room, searching frantically for Alyssa and Amanda. Amanda ran over and tried to grab her younger sister. But her hand went right through Anne's arm.

"Alyssa! Amanda!" cried Carrie. She ran into the kitchen and continued searching for her friends. "I thought you said you left them here!" she yelled to Anne.

"I did!" Anne replied. Tears started to spill from her eyes. "Where are they?"

"Anne! Carrie!" Alyssa shouted. "We're here!"

Alyssa stood in front of Anne, so close she could feel her warm breath. She waved and flung her arms around wildly while screaming into her sister's ear. But no matter how loudly Alyssa and Amanda shouted, it was useless—Anne and Carrie could not see or hear them. When she did gaze in their direction, Anne looked right through her two older sisters.

Alyssa looked at the Goodwins with pleading eyes. They stood silently, shaking their heads. It was no use. The curse was too strong. Alyssa and Amanda stopped moving and yelling as they watched Anne and Carrie walk out the door and into the night—back to the Petersons' home.

"You cannot communicate with the outside world," Mrs. Goodwin said. "In time, you may learn how to send whispers across the meadow, show your shadow to those outside the house, or even open and close the doors and shutters. But there will be no significant contact."

"Until New Year's Eve in fifty years," Alyssa said. "When we find our replacements."

EPILOGUE

December 27th

The rain poured down angrily on the old roof. The two sisters looked out of dingy window and watched the water splash against the glass. Amanda gazed longingly at the lush meadow in front of her; it separated the house she was in from the house next door. It was winter in Glory, Texas, and wildflowers were in bloom.

"You'll get to see them close-up soon enough," Alyssa told her sister.

"Hmm," Amanda replied. She was hardly listening.

"I thought you'd be more excited," Alyssa replied. "After all, think of all the things we'll see on the other side. There must be so many changes, and we're still so young. Who knows? Maybe we can find everyone again."

Amanda walked over to the faded sofa. She opened a book she'd already read a million times, flipping through the pages and not really reading any of the words.

"Seriously, why aren't you more excited?" Alyssa asked.

"I'm just not convinced that it's fair," Amanda said. "Think about it. We didn't have a choice."

Alyssa looked away from the window and then walked over to join her sister on the sofa.

"I just can't stay here anymore," Alyssa said. "We have to do it. We have to move forward with the plan!"

"How do we know that all will be okay?" Amanda asked her.

"It just will," Alyssa replied. "And we know that it will work. It did with us." And with that, Alyssa stood up anxiously. She couldn't bear the thought of her sister backing out of the plan now. They had waited so long, and she didn't want to face the outside world alone. They were destined to face it together. The house next door had remained empty for many, many years. Then one day last year, the FOR SALE sign was removed, and the girls excitedly watched a family moving boxes into it—a family with four teenage boys.

The girls had known then that their turn was upon them. Alyssa went back to the window. The rain had lifted and was now just pitter-pattering on the grass.

"Don't you want to be out there again?" Alyssa asked pointing to the fields. "We've waited long enough!"

Amanda rose from the sofa and then walked over to the window. She wrote an *A* in the foggy glass. "I guess we should try."

Alyssa grabbed Amanda's hand. "That's what I want to hear. Come on. We only have a few days, and there's still so much to be done. Timing is everything."

DO NOT FEAR—
WE HAVE ANOTHER CREEPY TALE FOR YOU!

CONTINUE READING FOR A SNEAK PEEK AT

You're invited to a

CREEPOVER™

Your Worst Nightmare

"You don't have to wait, Mom," Kristi Chen said firmly.

Mrs. Chen pursed her lips. "Are you sure, honey?" she asked. "It looks like the other parents are staying until the buses leave."

"But don't you have an important meeting?" Kristi replied.

"Yes," Mrs. Chen admitted. As one of the busiest lawyers in the state, Mrs. Chen was always rushing off to a big meeting or a court date.

"So go!" Kristi exclaimed. "Seriously, why waste your time standing around breathing in bus fumes?"

"Okay," Mrs. Chen finally gave in. She wrapped her arms around Kristi for a big hug. "Be careful, Kristi.

Don't go off by yourself; listen to your teachers; stay safe."

"Okay, Mom! Love you! Bye!" Kristi cried. She grabbed her overnight bag and backpack and bolted from the car before her mom could change her mind.

The rest of the seventh graders at Jefferson Middle School milled around the two buses that were idling by the curb. Kristi had never seen her classmates so excited to be at school on a Monday morning. She adjusted her backpack as she moved toward the crowd, looking for her best friend, Olivia Papas. But, as usual, Olivia found Kristi first.

"Kristi!" Olivia shrieked. "Are you psyched? I can't believe we're finally going on the field trip!"

"I know!" Kristi replied with a grin. Then she heard a familiar voice call out.

"Olivia! Kristi!"

Olivia's smile immediately disappeared. She grabbed Kristi's arm and dragged her around to the other side of the bus. "Oh, no. It's my parents . . ."

"Pretty bad this morning?" Kristi said sympathetically.

"The worst ever." Olivia groaned. "They brought the video camera and they're *interviewing* kids about the trip. I'm gonna die of embarrassment."

Kristi couldn't help laughing. "I'm sorry," she said. "That's rough. But look on the bright side—at least they're not chaperoning."

"Shhh!" Olivia said, her eyes wide. "Don't jinx it. Besides, I won't believe that until the buses are moving and I *know* they're not on them! How'd you get rid of your mom?"

Kristi shrugged. "She had a meeting. The usual."

"Lucky," Olivia replied. "I wish my parents had a life . . . outside of ruining mine."

Just then the girls heard a loud whistle. "Attention, seventh graders," Mr. Tanaka, their social studies teacher, called above all the noise. "Please join me by the flagpole."

Everyone hurried over toward Mr. Tanaka. Ms. Pierce, the science teacher, stood next to him.

"At last, it's the day we've all been waiting for," Mr. Tanaka announced. "The annual seventh-grade overnight field trip to Ravensburg Caverns is finally here. If you haven't already done so, please leave your luggage by the side of the bus so Mr. Carlson and Mr. Reed can load it. Remember, you can keep your backpack with you, but no eating or drinking on the buses—we'll stop for lunch when we're halfway to the caverns."

"I'd like to remind everyone that even though we'll be away from school for two days, the regular school rules are still in effect," Ms. Pierce added. "If you break those rules, you *will* be sent home immediately."

Mr. Tanaka eyed the kids sternly for a moment, then he smiled. "Okay! If you're on bus one, please follow me. If you're on bus two, go with Ms. Pierce. And let's get this show on the road!"

"Hurry," Kristi said to Olivia. "I want to get a good seat. In the back."

The girls pushed their way through the crowd to bus one—but Mr. and Mrs. Papas stepped in front of them.

"One more hug!" Mrs. Papas cried as she reached for Olivia.

Olivia rolled her eyes as her parents squashed her in a giant bear hug, but only Kristi could see.

"We're going to miss you so much, Poodle," Mr. Papas said.

"Dad. You promised you would stop calling me that," Olivia said through gritted teeth. The nickname had been stuck to Olivia since second grade, when she used to wear her curly black hair in two enormous, fluffy pigtails.

"Sorry." Mr. Papas apologized as he gave Olivia's ponytail a little tug. He turned to Kristi. "Take good care of each other, okay, Kristi?"

"Absolutely, Mr. Papas. You can count on me," Kristi said, trying not to laugh. "But we'd better go."

"I'm so bad at good-byes," Mrs. Papas said, wiping her eyes. "I love you, sweetie. Please be careful in the caves. I'm going to be so worried about you."

"Come on, Mom, I'll be back tomorrow night. You won't even notice I'm gone," Olivia replied. "Bye!" Then she hurried off to the bus, dragging Kristi behind her.

On the bus, Kristi spotted an empty row of seats that was almost at the back.

"Kristi, Kristi, wait," Olivia said, pulling Kristi over to a row on the opposite side of the bus—and right near the front. "Let's sit here."

"Here? In the front? Why?"

"Because my parents are taking pictures on the other side," Olivia explained. "They won't be able to see us if we sit over here. Please, Kristi? Please?"

Kristi sighed as she followed Olivia into the other

row. Now they would be sitting just two rows behind Mr. Tanaka. It seemed pretty silly to Kristi to pick a seat for the entire bus ride just because Olivia's parents wanted to take a couple of pictures of the bus leaving. But she knew how sensitive Olivia was about her parents, and how smothering they could be.

Olivia dug around in her backpack and pulled out her bright pink hairbrush. "Want me to do your hair?" she asked.

"Yes, please," Kristi replied. She twisted around in the seat so that her back was facing Olivia. Kristi closed her eyes as Olivia started brushing her hair.

An obnoxiously loud voice rang through the bus. "Hey, look at that! Usually the poodle is the one being groomed!"

Kristi didn't need to open her eyes to know who was talking. She'd know that voice anywhere. "Hi, Bobby," she said.

"Actually, what she meant to say was, 'Shut up, Bobby,'" Olivia said.

But Bobby Lehman had never shut up in his life, and he wasn't about to start now. He threw his backpack into the seat in front of Kristi and Olivia. "Ooh, Olivia, will you do my hair next? Puh-leeease?" Bobby cooed in a high-pitched, squeaky voice.

Olivia shot Bobby a dirty look as she put down her hairbrush and started playing around with her phone. Almost immediately, Kristi's phone buzzed with a text from Olivia.

K, u were so right about the seats. I wish we weren't stuck behind bobby. UGH

Kristi gave Olivia a little smile, but she didn't text her back. She knew Bobby could be really annoying. He was so desperate to be the center of attention all the time that it often backfired, and Kristi felt a little sorry for him. Kristi never would have admitted it—not even to Olivia—but she actually thought Bobby was cute. Kinda. Sorta. And sometimes he was actually really funny. And when he wasn't trying to show off, Kristi thought he could be really nice, too.

"So are you guys looking forward to exploring the caves tomorrow?" Bobby continued as the bus pulled out of the school parking lot.

Olivia put on some headphones and started listening

to music from her phone. There was no way that Bobby could've missed the hint, but he ignored it completely.

"I'm not," Bobby answered his own question. "Those caves are scary. Not fun scary, *really* scary."

"What do you mean?" Kristi asked curiously.

"My brothers told me all about it," Bobby said loudly. "They said it should be *criminal* to take kids into the Ravensburg Caverns. After what happened there."

Kristi raised her eyebrows. She was pretty sure that Bobby was about to tell one of his over-the-top stories. But even so, she couldn't help asking, "What? What happened?"

"It was a long time ago," Bobby began as kids in other seats stopped chatting and started listening in. "Almost a hundred years ago, actually. Well, the caves were a really big deal even back then. Like, every day people lined up for a chance to go inside and see the wonders of the Ravensburg Caverns. And schools—just like our school—sent kids there on field trips."

"So?" yelled Evan Hollis from a few rows behind Kristi.

"So . . . ," Bobby said, pausing dramatically, "so . . . one time a class disappeared in the caves. Twenty-one kids. Vanished. Gone without a trace."

Now it seemed like just about everyone on the bus was focused on Bobby. Even Mr. Tanaka had shifted in his seat, like he was listening with one ear.

"The townspeople searched for *months*," Bobby said, leaning over the seat back. He had everyone's attention now and he was determined to keep it. "Even after they had lost all hope that the kids would be found alive, they kept looking. They brought in search-and-rescue dogs and they searched, and they searched . . . and they found nothing. Not a footprint. Not a fingerprint. Not a sweater. Not a hair bow. Not a body. Not even a bone. Twenty-one kids vanished off the face of the earth, as if they had never . . . even . . . existed."

"But what . . ." Kristi swallowed; her mouth was suddenly very dry. She tried again. "But what happened to them?"

Bobby shrugged. "Nobody knows. Most people think that they must have fallen into, like, an abyss or something. Some of those drops in the cave . . . Even now, they don't know quite how far they go down. But I don't think so."

"How come?" asked Olivia. Kristi wondered when she'd taken off her headphones.

"Come on," Bobby said confidently. "How would twenty-one kids all fall down the same hole? I mean, sure, two or three. Maybe even five. But wouldn't the ones at the back be able to save themselves? They weren't, like, babies. They were our age. So whatever happened to those kids was worse. Way worse. And my brother says . . ."

"What?" Kristi and Olivia exclaimed at the same time.

"My brother says that if you listen really carefully in the caves, you can still hear the echoes of their cries for help. *Please . . . please . . . please . . . help . . . help . . . help . . . meeeee . . . meeeee . . . meeeee . . . .*," Bobby said, raising his voice to a shrill whisper as he imitated the echoes.

The sound of Bobby's echoes made chills run down Kristi's neck. But apparently she was the only one who responded that way: Everyone else on the bus burst into laughter. It was definitely not the response Bobby was hoping for. His whole face darkened.

"Okay, okay, save it for Halloween, Mr. Lehman," Mr. Tanaka said sternly. "An excellent tall tale . . . but not a true one. You'll all learn about the real history of the Ravensburg Caverns on our tour tomorrow."

"It *is* true," Bobby said stubbornly. "I know a lot more about the caverns than you do."

"Watch it, young man," Mr. Tanaka said, and there was no mistaking the warning in his voice. "And face forward, please. No turning around in your seat while the bus is moving—you know better."

Bobby slumped down in his seat. Kristi couldn't see him any longer, but she could imagine the frustrated look on his face. Just then her phone buzzed with another text:

Lame story, right?

Kristy half-smiled, half-shrugged at Olivia.

She couldn't stop thinking about the story that Bobby had told. The thought of being lost in the caves . . . lost forever . . . made her wish that she was in second-period Spanish class instead of heading straight for the Ravensburg Caverns. Because you could use a lot of words to describe Bobby—he was definitely a loudmouth, a bragger, an attention hog—but Kristi knew one thing: Bobby Lehman had never looked so serious . . . or more like he was telling the truth.

WANT MORE CREEPINESS?

Then you're in luck, because P. J. Night has
some more scares for you and your friends!

A book cipher is a special code that can only be
cracked with the help of a book. Each set of numbers
in the list below represents one word that appears
somewhere in this book. The first number is a page
in the book, the second number is a line on that
page, and the third number is a word in that line.

For example, to decode 32-7-2, go to page 32,
find the 7th line down on that page, and then read
the 2nd word in that line. Did you get "knowing"?
If so, you've got it!

Now can you crack the book cipher below to read the fine print in the Goodwins' deed? Fill in the corresponding word on each blank.

30-1-3 _____

130-19-9 _____

5-8-7 _____

131-2-6 _____

28-22-7 _____

45-13-2 _____

61-21-1 _____

8-23-8 _____

9-3-11 _____

70-20-6 _____

63-13-2 _____

23-11-7 _____

35-8-5 _____

84-18-2 _____

84-18-6 _____

105-6-8 _____

10-5-1 _____

106-15-4 _____

YOU'RE INVITED TO . . .
CREATE YOUR OWN SCARY STORY!

Do you want to turn your sleepover into a creepover? Telling a spooky story is a great way to set the mood. P. J. Night has written a few sentences to get you started. Fill in the rest of the story and have fun scaring your friends.

You can also collaborate with your friends on this story by taking turns. Have everyone at your sleepover sit in a circle. Pick one person to start. She will add a sentence or two to the story, cover what she wrote with a piece of paper leaving only the last word or phrase visible, and then pass the story to the next girl. Once everyone has taken a turn, read the scary story you created together aloud!

> Carrie was so excited for her first day of seventh grade. She was digging around in her backpack for her cell phone when the bus stopped in front of a creepy, old, abandoned house. To her surprise, a tall, pale boy wearing strange clothes got on the bus

and sat down in the empty seat beside her.
She was about to ask if he was new to town
when he turned to her and said ...

_____

_____

_____

_____

_____

_____

_____

_____

_____

_____

_____

_____

_____

_____

_____

_____

_____

_____

THE END

A lifelong night owl, **P. J. NIGHT** often works furiously into the wee hours of the morning, writing down spooky tales and dreaming up new stories of the supernatural and otherworldly. Although P. J.'s whereabouts are unknown at this time, we suspect the author lives in a drafty, old mansion where the floorboards creak when no one is there and the flickering candlelight creates shadows that creep along the walls. We truly wish we could tell you more, but we've been sworn to keep P. J.'s identity a secret . . . and it's a secret we will take to our graves!